Arrange Us

KATY REGNERY

Please visit my website at **www.katyregnery.com**
Editor: Tessa Shapcott
Proofreader: Julie Deaton
Formatter: CookieLynn Publishing Services
Cover Designer: Katy Regnery

First Edition: May 2019
Arrange Us: a novel / by Katy Regnery—1st ed.
ISBN: 978-1-944810-44-3

My name is Courtney Jane Salinger...
and I just got married.

I was sick of Netflix and chilling, hanging out, catfishing, ghosting,
break-ups, make-ups, and games.

So, what did I do?

I signed up with a married-at-first-sight matchmaking service,
and I married the man who was waiting for me at the altar.

We did it.
We're married.
He's mine.
I'm his.
Man and wife.
Missus and Mister.

Except...
We barely know each other.
We've never lived together.

Turns out I'm an early bird, and he's a night owl.
He works nights and I work all day.
His parents keep asking when we're having kids,
while mine keep emailing me the names of divorce lawyers.
Women everywhere want to get in his pants, including
his omnipresent ex ... and my newly-single boss can't seem
to get the hint that I am off the market.

No one thinks we can make it.
And now I'm starting to wonder too.

Being arranged was just the beginning.
Is happily-ever-after even possible?

For Callie and Henry.
Thank you for always reminding me of what matters most.
Dawn, thank you for reading.

xoxo

Arrange Us

PROLOGUE
December 15th

"You've reached Josh Dalton. Please leave a message."

I let the phone fall from my ear just as the door to the inner office opens.

An older gentleman, whom I assume to be Dr. Daniel Scott, Marriage Counselor, leans against the doorframe, scans the waiting room, then looks at me with concern.

"He's not here yet, huh?"

My phone is still in my hand. "I keep getting his voice mail."

"Mrs. Dalton, do you think he's still coming?"

No, I don't.

"I don't know," I whisper.

"We've waited for nearly half an hour. Perhaps we should reschedule? For after the holidays?"

"I'm so sorry," I say, standing from the waiting room guest chair and gathering my things together. Tears burn my eyes, but I blink them back. "Please bill me for the inconvenience, Dr. Scott. We—*I* didn't mean to waste your time."

"You haven't." His eyes are kind, sympathetic. He tilts his head to the side as he scans my face. "Technically, you still have half an hour left. Do *you* want to come in for a moment and chat with me?"

The receptionist, who's been sitting at her desk with her coat on since I arrived, sighs loudly.

"Dawn-Marie," says Dr. Scott, glancing at her over my shoulder, "I don't see any reason for you to stay. Why don't you go now? I'll speak to Mrs. Dalton for a few minutes, and then I can lock up. Have a nice—"

"Thank you, Dr. Scott!" she says, leaping from her chair and halfway out the door before he can finish wishing her a nice weekend.

"Come in, Mrs. Dalton," says the therapist, opening his office door for me. "My wife's not expecting me until five o'clock. Enough time for a short chat, huh?"

I follow him into his office, which is very simple, and monochromatically soothing.

An off-white couch with tan pillows sits to my right, and a tan leather easy chair is positioned across the cream-colored carpet, with a simple, glass coffee table in the center. A desk sits in the back corner of the office surrounded by bookshelves, but Dr. Scott takes a seat in the chair and gestures for me to sit on the couch.

"Was your husband ...in agreement? About this course of action? Therapy, I mean?"

Hot tears slide down my cheeks, and I shrug pathetically.

"Mrs. Dalton," he says, tenting his fingers under his nose and leaning forward in his chair, "may I be blunt? You seem miserable. And I hate to see *anyone* miserable, especially at Christmastime. Is there any way you could get me up to speed in a nutshell? Maybe spend fifteen minutes on the history of your marriage and then tell me what's been going on recently? I'd like to try to help you make sense of it if I can."

A nutshell, I think. *How do you compress six months of a mostly-arranged marriage into a fifteen-minute nutshell? How do you take the highs and lows, the ups and downs, the marvelous and the heartbreaking and give them all equal time? And how do you tell this man with kind, sympathetic, well-meaning eyes that you haven't the slightest hope that he can help you?*

"Maybe just start at the beginning?" he suggests.

"There were two beginnings," I say softly, taking a tissue to wipe my cheeks and meeting his eyes with mine. "One in a bar. And another in Scotland."

"You met at a bar?"

I nod.

"And you met again in Scotland?"

"We were married there."

"Then start there. In Scotland."

I look down at my hands in my lap, staring, for a moment, at the two rings on the fourth finger of my left hand. One is a gold band with a small, emerald-cut garnet. The other is a simple gold wedding band. The sight of them together makes me want to weep.

In my mind, I can see a snapshot of me today: a frozen image of Courtney Dalton sitting across from a marriage counselor with very little hope in her swiftly breaking heart. But somewhere in my head, a rewind button is pressed, and in an instant, I see six months of *us*—a montage of me and

Josh—fly across the screen of my consciousness like a movie played backward.

And when it ends, there's a different snapshot altogether.

It's from six months ago, and it's a picture of me and Josh holding hands in front of a plate glass window at Inverness Airport. There's a storm approaching in the distance, and our wild, wonderful honeymoon has just crashed to a sorry end.

A harbinger of all that came next? Possibly...

And yet, those hands are clasped tightly, and in my mind, we appear a united front against whatever may befall us, whatever waits for us back in New York.

My mind skitters to those first few days and my heart clenches. Moving boxes. A shared home. A shared bed.

It wasn't all bad. Not at all. So much of the past six months was good. So much of it was heaven. It was challenging, for sure, and we made mistakes, but we learned so much. It seemed—*I felt so sure*—that we would make it. There were tiny miracles everywhere, at every turn. There was fun. There was growth. Real, measurable growth.

And there was love, wasn't there?

I was so very certain that there was *true love*.

I gulp over the giant lump in my throat and raise my eyes to Dr. Scott.

"It all started in June," I begin, "when my husband and I were...*arranged*."

CHAPTER 1

Six months ago

<u>Courtney</u>

Something else I have learned about my husband today:

He is able to sleep soundly . . . right, smack in the middle of a crisis.

Somewhere over Ireland, while I was in the bathroom, Josh fell asleep. And I mean, *really and truly* asleep. He's snoring softly when I return to my roomy business-class seat.

For a second, I stare at him in amazement, fighting the impulse to run to the galley for a glass of cold water and throw it in his face. Instead, I sit down in my seat with a terse sigh, purposely knocking his elbow off of our shared armrest. Checking to see if it woke him up, I'm disappointed to see that it didn't, but grudgingly decide to let him sleep. I can use this time to think. Lord knows there's a shit ton of unpleasantness to sort out.

My father's voice message, which I listened to in the airport at Inverness, is singed onto my brain, and I turn my thoughts to it, reviewing the words in my head:

Well, you really screwed the pooch this time, CJ. Married? To a practical stranger? In a foreign country? It reeks of shame. It reeks of a coverup. Are you knocked up? Are you in trouble? Well, miss, until your mother and I have been given the goddamned respect due to us by our only daughter, and been apprised of the meaning behind this—this fiasco, you're out. You're a stranger to us. You're—you're not the girl we raised. Do you hear me? Have some decency and call your goddamned mother. Now!

I take a wobbly breath, looking across my husband and out the window. All gray and white as far as I can see, it's clear we're in the clouds, but far from heaven.

Why did Aunt Lucy tell my father? What purpose did it serve? They're furious with me and they have a right to be hurt. I am, after all, their only child. And I did, after all, elope with a relative stranger. They only met Josh once at a wedding last month, and at the time, I made it clear to my father that there was no future for us. There was no courtship, no engagement, no wedding planning, no easing them into the reality of my nuptials. No allowing them the chance to celebrate their daughter's engagement or marriage with their friends. I can see how they'd feel snubbed. They have a right to be angry.

I rub my forehead, which is aching, and resolve to think about it once we touch down in New York. I'll call them in a day or two and make plans for Josh and me to go out to Greenwich and explain everything. Hopefully, they'll be accepting, but the grim reality is that they will have to come to terms with my marriage. The deed is done. We said our "I do"s, we honeymooned in Scotland, and the multiple orgasms I had this week speak to the fact that our union has been thoroughly consummated. We are *very* married, whether they like it or not.

Picking up my glass, I polish off the rest of my champagne. I turn my eyes to Josh, feeling my whole face soften as I scan his handsomeness. My lips tip up involuntarily. I haven't watched him like this very much this week: sleeping peacefully.

His dark brown hair has grown out during his several weeks in England, and it curls softly at the ends, making him look younger than twenty-six. He has an insanely sexy five o-clock shadow darkening his strong jawline. His lips, full and pink, are slack with sleep, and his long, dark eyelashes practically dust the high planes of his cheeks. He is stupendously beautiful by any standards, and he belongs to me.

Something deep within me quickens, desperate for the feel of his body surging inside of mine. Muscle memories make my pussy walls clench, and I dart a quick glance at the lavatory not ten feet in front of us. Should I wake him up? Would I dare? Would he?

"Miss, would you like the sandwich or the salad for your tea?"

As though I've been caught doing something devious, I feel my cheeks flush with surprise and embarrassment as the flight attendant waits for my reply. When I look up at her, I realize we're about the same age, but she's much thinner and taller than me, with icy blonde hair and perfect makeup. Slick red fingernails glisten against the passenger manifest she holds in her hands. I bet she can get any man who catches her eye…

"Um. The, uh, salad, please."

…and *her eye* has landed on what's mine.

She grins at Josh and asks, "What do you think he wants?"

As she ogles my husband, my feelings are split in two. Half of me likes it that he's so hot, strange women can't help gawking at him. The other half is scared beyond belief that such interest may lead to him leaving me someday.

"My *husband* would prefer a sandwich," I say, with the slightest edge in my voice.

"You're married? To *him*?" she says, her eyes widening as they snap back to my face.

"Last weekend," I say, holding up my ringed hand and waggling my fingers.

"Congratulations," she says, her face cooling from interested to professional.

"Out of curiosity," I say, "why didn't you think we were together?"

"I just . . . didn't realize," she says, looking uncomfortable. Glancing down at the paper in her hands, she relaxes. "Your surnames are different." She gives me a small, almost apologetic, smile. "I'll be back with your salad soon, ma'am."

As she steps away to take the orders of the passengers seated in 2A and 2B, I'm left feeling insecure. Was that the truth? She didn't think we were together because our last names were different on the passenger list? Or was it that Josh is so much more handsome than I am pretty? I suspect the latter and it makes my stomach roil.

I think about our argument in the airport earlier, when I told Josh he didn't have to go back to work at Tidewaters if he didn't want to; about how I could support us both. He was so firm in his desire to return to work, to bring home a paycheck, though he must know that whatever he makes will only be a fraction of my salary. We don't need the money he makes to live comfortably, and wouldn't his time be better served concentrating on his plays?

I look over my shoulder at Miss-Hottie-Pants-Stewardess and my heart clenches.

If I'm honest, my worries about him returning to work as a bartender don't have anything to do with my salary or his convenience. I know the way women look at him and I know how alcohol emboldens them to proposition him. I've watched it happen many times since first meeting Josh. My *real* reason for wanting to financially support us both is that I don't trust other women around my husband. Or maybe—just maybe, though I've no real cause to doubt him—I don't trust Josh yet.

That thought sits uncomfortably with me.

I don't like it.

I want to trust my husband.

At least until he gives me a reason not to.

But I have no history to comfort me. We haven't dated really. I mean, we've gone out on a few dates, but under the guise of friendship. We were never boyfriend and girlfriend.

We didn't spend months in each other's company, learning about how each other handles unwanted flirtation, and finding comfort in watching the way it's deflected. We didn't build a foundation of trust based on shared experiences and time spent together. We went from friends to spouses to lovers in the space of a month.

It occurs to me that I have no idea how Josh behaves as a boyfriend, let alone a husband. Will he still flirt with the customers at Tidewaters even though he's in a committed relationship? In the face of my objections, would he call the flirting "harmless," even though it will make me feel insecure and jealous to see it?

Am I borrowing troubles that don't yet belong to me?

Yes.

Why?

Because there is so much unknown between my husband and me, and the pre-wedding recommendations of my "experts"—to be optimistic, to build a strong friendship, and to take my time—feel useless right now. Yes, I want to be optimistic, and yes, I want to build a strong friendship with my husband. But I also want to trust him. I want to feel secure in our marriage. Call it "only-child syndrome," or blame it on the fact that I grew up privileged-yet-ignored; but I want to be the most important person in Josh's life.

I lift my glass when another flight attendant stops by with a bottle of champagne. I don't want to think about my parents' disapproval, and I don't want to think about Josh going back to work at Tidewaters. I down the champagne and raise the glass again, despite the raised eyebrow of the man pouring it.

"Would ye like the bottle?" he asks with a bit of Scottish sass.

I give him a look that would whither heather, and he backs away slowly.

I wish I had a guidebook for this.

A Handy Guide for the Newly Married, I think.

No. Better yet:

A Handy Guide for Newly-Arranged Newlyweds.

That would be perfect.

Hmm. I pull my iPad from the pocket on the seat back in front of me and power it on, quickly signing into the airlines' wi-fi. There's a book for every other topic under the sun. Might there be one for this too?

I open my internet browser and head over to Amazon. When the storefront comes up, I type in: Newlywed Book. First up? Two cookbooks, which are gorgeous but not helpful, and a cute-looking book by Caroline Tiger called *The Newlywed's Instruction Manual*. It's completely adorable, and I buy a paperback copy right away, but I am fairly certain it's not exactly what I'm looking for right now.

I have an idea! Maybe one of our experts wrote a book about being married at first sight. My heart beats faster with hope. After all, that's what they're known for, right?

Typing in "Sydney Morningstar, MD," I'm gratified when a list of books appears a moment later, the first of which—*You've Been Married at First Sight! Now What?*—speaks exactly to my concerns. I download the book onto my iPad, waiting a moment for it to download.

Just as the flight attendant swings back to fill up my champagne glass again—this time, without comment or sass— the book appears on my Kindle app, ready to read.

I swipe it open to the table of contents and scan the ten chapter headers: Moving In, In-Laws, Finances, Social Life, Exes, Trust, Celebrations, Communication, Conflict & Resolution, and The Future.

With a sigh of relief, I swipe to the Foreword, written by one of our other *Arrange Me* experts, Pastor Kenneth Harrison, and settle into my seat to read.

***

<u>Josh</u>

When I wake up, I glance to my right to find Courtney dozing beside me, and my heart swells with so much affection for her, it's baffling to me that we've only been married for a week.

Do I love Courtney?

My actions—flying to England to marry her so that no one else could—might speak to the fact that I do, but I'm not ready to say the words yet. I care about her deeply. I want to smash in the face of anyone who makes her cry. She belongs to me now, and I belong to her, in a very real and official way. But love? I don't know. I just don't know yet.

Maybe it's because I haven't had a ton of experience with romantic love.

I thought I was in love with my high school girlfriend, Liliana, but in retrospect, I can see that what we felt for each other was puppy love: a deep, and incredibly intense, infatuation.

I had a few girlfriends in college and after, but I was never in love with any of them, and that includes Sam.

Sam.

I feel a pit in the bottom of my stomach when I think about the texts she sent me while I was on my honeymoon. Checking to be sure that Courtney's still asleep, I lean forward and pull my phone from my back pocket. Then, angling myself against the window, I re-read my ex-girlfriend's messages.

Text #1: *Max and I broke up. I need you. I really need you, Josh. Please call me.*

Text #2: *Josh, please don't get married. Please. I'm begging you. I should have said something in New York, that morning on your bed when we were talking, but I got scared. Call me before you go through with it. I can't be too late. I can't be.*

Text #3: *Another day goes by and I haven't heard a word from you and I'm so scared that you're not getting my messages. Just in case it matters to you, I want you to know how I feel about you. I love you. I LOVE YOU, JOSH DALTON. Not just as a roommate or a friend. I've been in love with you since NYU. When we broke up, I kept hoping you'd come back to me, that you'd give me another chance. When you didn't, I got together with Max to make you jealous. And then…I don't know…we stayed together because he was nice to me and at least I wasn't alone. And then you moved into the apartment with us, and I could see you every day, and I just hoped that sometime, someday, someway, you'd SEE me again. You'd fall for me again. You'd forgive me. I had this fantasy that we'd be brushing our*

Text #4: *teeth or you'd sit next to me on your bed to watch New Girl, and suddenly you'd just know—you'd remember the good times we had and you'd want me again, and once you wanted me, I'd let it build and build until you couldn't stand it anymore. Finally, you'd tell me that you'd fallen in love with me again—or that you'd never fallen out of love in the first place—and I'd break up with Max and he'd be okay with it, because he and I are probably better off as friends, and you and I would be together. And I swear to God, I'd never cheat on you again, Josh. I swear on my life we'd be happy. We'd be madly in love and work on our plays, and someday we'd see them produced side by side. It's you and me, Josh. It always was. Don't you see that? Don't you know it's true?*

With a soft groan, I flip over the phone and rest it on my thigh, staring out the window.

No, I think. *No, I don't see that. No, I don't know it's true. And how fucked up is it that you were only with Max to make me jealous, Sam?*

I clench my jaw with annoyance, thinking back on my checkered history with Sam. We were close friends in college and started dating just after graduation when we were both chosen as playwrights-in-residence at the New Dramatists. Over the summer, we even shared the spare bedroom there, looking around for part-time jobs in the same restaurant and an apartment we could afford together in Manhattan.

We never found either.

Sam started tutoring and was invited to share an apartment in Queens with some girls she knew from college. I took a job at a downtown bar and moved into a rental house on Staten Island with my friend, Mike, and some of the musicians in his band. Gradually, our relationship fizzled, the two-hour bus commute from Flushing to Elm Park taking a toll on our time and wallets.

Well, that, I think, *and the fact that Sam cheated on me.*

Toward the end of our relationship, she called me late at work one night, sobbing and incoherent, telling me all about how she'd had sex with some guy, who was the friend of her roommate's brother, and how sorry she was. It had taken me a few minutes to piece together what she was saying, but once I understood the intent of her call: to apologize for cheating on me and ask for forgiveness, I was done.

Cheating's a hard no for me. Always has been. Always will be.

The next day we met in Central Park, near the statue of Alice, and we said our goodbyes. She wept continuously. I may have shed a tear or two as well, but honestly, I was more hurt by the betrayal than anything else. I wasn't in love with her, and even if I'd been willing to keep dating her, to see if love developed, the cheating killed our chances at any sort of happiness together. I couldn't see her the same way anymore. I couldn't trust her. We could try to get our friendship back on track, because we had history, but love?

No way. I'm not that stupid. Once a cheater, always a cheater. And I'm no masochist with my heart.

"Excuse me, sir. You were asleep during the tea service, but I saved a sandwich for you."

I look up to see a flight attendant standing in the aisle next to Courtney.

"Oh, great. Thanks."

Her expression warms, her smile widens. After working in bars for as long as I have, I know what's coming next. *And 3...2...1...*

"And what can I get you to drink? Coffee? Tea? Me?"

There we go.

She giggles softly, like maybe she's just kidding, but also leaving the door open for me to wonder if she's not. I keep my expression impassive.

"What was my wife drinking?" I ask, putting a little extra oomph on the word "wife."

She leans back a touch. "Champagne."

"Then I'll have the same."

Her "come-hither" look fades into a professional half-smile. "Of course. I'll be right back with your meal."

I grab my phone from where it's resting and pull down my tray table. With a long sigh, I look at Sam's last couple of messages.

Text #5: *It's been two weeks. I'm guessing you went through with it. Fuck, Josh. Why didn't you call me? Fuck, fuck, fuck. Why are you such an unforgiving bastard? Why couldn't you give me another chance?*

Text #6: *Call me when you get home. I don't care if you're married. We still need to talk about everything.*

"Here we are! Ham and cheddar sandwich and a glass of champagne."

"Thanks," I say, tucking my phone into the seat pocket and draping my napkin across my lap. I've never sat in business class before, but my drink is served in a stemmed glass, not a plastic cup, and the food is served on china with heavy silverware. It's pretty decadent, and as much as I'm enjoying it, it also reminds me of the disparity between Courtney's and my lifestyles.

Earlier today, when we were talking about our return to New York, it bugged me that she offered to support me. Why did it bother me so much?

Maybe because my mom never had to support my dad. He was the breadwinner from the start, and it sort of solidified those gender roles in my head. It feels wrong—like mooching—to let my wife support me. I don't like it. Even if I can only contribute a fraction of what she can, I'd still like to do my part.

Opening a text box, I send a quick message to Lulu, my boss at Tidewaters, telling her that I'm moving in with Courtney this weekend, but that I'm happy to start working again next week. As I put my phone back down, it occurs to me that if Courtney's in Japan from Monday to Thursday, and I work on Thursday, Friday, and Sunday, we won't see much of each other when she finally gets home. I make a mental note to ask Lulu if I can change up my hours a little and take weekday shifts instead. Tips won't be as good Monday to Thursday, but if I can get weekends free, my bride and I can spend them together.

Compromises, right? Marriage is all about compromises, and I'm ready to make some.

I take a bite of my sandwich and wash it down with champagne, which is a surprisingly good combination, then glance over at Courtney as she sighs in her sleep. On her lap is an iPad, and I pick it up gently, turning it over and powering it on.

It looks like she was reading a book before she drifted off, and a few keystrokes gives me the title: *You've Been Married at First Sight! Now What?* She's currently on Chapter 2, entitled In-Laws, and as I finish my meal, I read a little bit.

Chapter 2

In-Laws.

Or more like Out-Laws!

With the way Hollywood likes to portray in-laws, it's not surprising if you greet this chapter with a grimace and shiver. That said, I will try to change your mind and widen your perspective, because in-laws can be awesome!

There's no reason why you can't have a close and loving relationship with your spouse's family. In fact, an affectionate bond with your in-laws can enrich your marriage more than you can possibly guess. So, let's dig in together and talk about how to create and nurture a lifelong friendship with your partner's family…

A mental image of William Salinger sails through my

head and I gingerly lay the iPad face-down on the bolster between me and his daughter.

Close and loving? Affectionate? Lifelong friendship?

Not likely, I think, remembering the look on Courtney's face as she was listening to a voice message from her father at the airport before our departure. She didn't want to talk about it much, but apparently, he threatened to disown her for marrying me, and it makes me want to throat-punch him for upsetting her. I promised to go out to Connecticut with her and talk to them, but I'm dreading it…almost as much as I'm dreading the hurt, disappointed tone in my own mother's voice when I tell her I eloped.

My mother is midwestern and traditional. She would have expected me to bring Courtney out to Minnetonka at least twice before proposing; preferably for Christmas and Easter. And I know my mom—she would have wanted to share baby pictures and recipes with Courtney and introduce her to all of the ladies on the vestry committee at church. She would have hosted a luncheon for Courtney and her lady friends and announced our engagement in the local newspaper. It's going to kill her that she missed our courtship, engagement, and wedding. To make up for it, Courtney and I are going to have to go out there soon.

Maybe for Thanksgiving, I think. *And maybe for Christmas too.*

It may not be possible for *me* to have a close and loving relationship with the cold, rich Salingers, but I know that my parents, especially my mother, will be eager to embrace Courtney.

In my mind, I see Courtney and my mother together, standing side by side, and feel my eyebrows furrow at the image. My mother, who is a little overweight and more than a little gray, wears mom-jeans and a frumpy, floral, short-sleeve top. Courtney, on the other hand, looks chic and sophisticated in a black cocktail dress, heels, and sunglasses.

Huh.

Yes, Courtney works on Wall Street and my mother is a housewife. And sure, Courtney has a master's degree and my mom dropped out of college to get married and have kids. It's true that baking and church attendance rank high on my mother's list of priorities and—hmm, actually, I have no idea if Courtney bakes or attends church or—

Shit. My mother and Courtney have zero in common. Nada. Nothing.

I switch the pictures in my mind and imagine my mother and Courtney's mother side by side. When I met Mrs. Salinger at a wedding last month, she looked fresh and young, with a smart blonde bob and a short, elegant dress that showed off tan, toned legs. As we foxtrotted around the country club ballroom, I learned that Miranda Salinger graduated from Vassar and got her MFA from Columbia.

Lord. I doubt Miranda Salinger and Joanie Dalton would have enough conversation between them to last half an hour.

Will Courtney think my parents are two hicks from the Midwest? Because it will really, really hurt my family's feelings if they feel rejected by my "big-city" wife.

I down the rest of my champagne and cover my

uneaten food with a napkin. I'm just not hungry anymore. Between dealing with Sam, anticipating our almost-opposite work schedules, and pondering the fact that Courtney will probably hate my family, I've lost my appetite.

How the hell did we ever think this could work?

How the fuck were we so naïve?

The plane suddenly jostles, but when my stomach drops, I'm pretty sure it has nothing to do with turbulence.

"Sir? Are you finished? I think we're about to encounter a bit of bumpy air, so I'd like to clear your tray, please."

I hand the tray to the flight attendant, listening as the captain makes an announcement telling all passengers to please buckle their seat belts and stay seated. Before I buckle in, I reach over and click Courtney's belt in place across her waist. The plane bounces again and as I lean away from her, her eyes flare open.

"What's going on?"

"Just a little turbulence," I say, reaching for the two ends of my belt and fastening it in place. "No big deal."

The plane drops again and suddenly a claw-like grip encircles my wrist. "I don't...I don't like turbulence."

I look up at my wife to find her eyes wide, her face white.

"You're afraid?"

She is staring straight ahead, sitting rigidly in her seat. "Yes."

I don't know why this surprises me, but it does. Big time. Courtney's a world traveler. She goes to Japan for two-day business trips. How could she be frightened of a little chop in the clouds?

"Baby," I say, peeling her talons from my wrist and clasping her hand in mine. "It's okay. It's nothing."

"It's not n-nothing. In 1997, t-turbulence led to the d-death of a passenger...on a United f-flight...um, f-from Narita," she whispers, her breathing jagged and shallow.

I don't know where Narita is, but Courtney hasn't offered me awkward facts like this since telling me that most people die of heart attacks on Mondays. It's a "tell." She's extremely upset.

Wishing the bolster wasn't separating us and I could pull her onto the safety of my lap, I say softly but firmly, "Give me your other hand."

I hold out my far hand, watching as she takes a moment to let go of the arm rest and grab it. She grips it so hard I wince, but I don't pull it away.

"Good. Now, look at me," I say.

Holding hands like this has angled our bodies toward one another and created a ring that includes only us.

"Her...she wasn't b-buckled," Courtney tells me. "The passenger. F-From Narita."

"I buckled you in," I say, as another pocket of air forces us to lift an inch from our seats before throwing us back down. "I buckled you before I buckled me. You're safe. I'll keep you safe."

"You c-can't," she says, licking her lips as the plane drops sharply, the sudden movement eliciting some panicked chatter from the passengers around us. "If the p-plane...if..."

"If the plane what?"

She gasps as we rise and fall again. "If it c-can't be c-controlled…"

Staring at the bright blue of my wife's eyes, I don't think about what I'm going to say next. The words have left my lips before I knew they were waiting to be said.

"If the plane goes down, I'll be looking at you. I'll be holding your hands. I'll be sitting next to you." I squeeze her hands lightly in mine. "I'll die happy because I got to marry you, Courtney. I got to call you my wife. I got to start this crazy, stupid, ridiculous, awesome adventure with you before I died."

Tears spring into her eyes as I speak, and she tilts her head to the side like she's processing my words.

"And you'll be looking at me, baby. You'll be sitting next to me, holding my hands. And hopefully you won't regret marrying me in Scotland. Hopefully, being married to each other, even for a short time, was worth it."

She sniffles as the bouncing tapers off, her eyes wet and luminous as she stares into mine. The captain assures us that the worst is past, and her grip eases just a little.

"I don't regret anything," she says. "But I'm scared."

"The turbulence is over," I say, glancing out the window to my right before meeting her eyes again.

Her gaze is steady and severe when she replies, "I think we both know it's just beginning."

She releases my right hand, but when she tries to let go of my left one, I won't let her. I hold on tighter.

"Look at me," I tell her. When she does, I say, "Then

keep looking at me. Keep holding my hand. Whatever happens next, we're married. I'm your husband and you're my wife. And wherever this crazy, stupid, ridiculous, awesome adventure leads us, we'll handle it together."

For the first time since we left the airport in Inverness, Courtney Jane Salinger Dalton smiles at me. It's a small smile at first, but it grows and grows until it takes over her lovely face and shines brightly from her tear-filled eyes.

"You mean it?" she asks me.

I know we have challenges up ahead: exes and moving in together, in-laws and celebrations and work schedules. I know that there will be fights and make-ups, anger and joy, ups and downs, highs and lows.

But I also feel like I can tackle *anything* if this woman is sitting beside me.

So, I smile back at her with as much confidence as I can muster. "I do."

CHAPTER 2
• MOVING IN •

"The thing about moving in together is that your space isn't your space anymore. And the most important single thing you can do is change your mindset from mine *to* ours.*"*

--Dr. Sydney Morningstar

<u>Josh</u>

No matter how many times Courtney says, "Make yourself at home," it's easier said than done.

My belongings, which we rescued from a small storage unit on Saturday morning, are meager: three suitcases of clothes, a box of shoes, a box of toiletries, a plastic storage container full of books and plays, an electric guitar that I won in a poker game (but don't know how to play), a dart board from my NYU dorm room that's seen better days, a computer tower, keyboard, mouse and monitor, a small, flat-screen TV, my parents' old DVD player, a small box of DVDs, and a blanket knitted for me by my grandmother before she died.

It's sort of a pathetic, ragtag collection of items, but the reality is that I've lived in three apartments since graduating from college, and all were furnished. I've had no need to buy a bed or sofa or kitchen utensils. Not to mention, on a budget like mine, you don't buy anything that you don't need. The previous tenant left behind a bed, mattress, two sets of sheets, a comforter, bedside table, and lamp? Awesome. I'm all set. The girls who just went on tour stocked the kitchen with second-hand cups, plates, cookery, and cutlery? Perfect. No need to get more.

Artists don't live like the rest of the population and we're okay with that. It's almost a right-of-passage to "make do" because you're "paying your dues" all the while. We live in squalor together. We show up on someone's opening night in a borrowed tux. And we know deep in our hearts that one day—*one day*—that success may be ours too.

So, my wife's apartment? Which, by the way, I'd never even seen until a taxi dropped us off there after we arrived in New York fresh from our honeymoon? It's like a *really* nice hotel room. No! A hotel *suite*. Wait. Back up. When you walk into her building, there's a doorman and a fancy elevator, the lobby smells like really expensive deodorant, and there's a crystal chandelier hanging over a Persian carpet. Then, there's Courtney's apartment. And it's deeee-luxe. Lots of New York apartments have hardwood floors, but her place has molding. *New* molding. Chair rail *and* crown, like you'd see in a super fancy hotel in London, thank you very much.

In her living room, which looks like something out of a catalog, the sofa matches the loveseat, easy chair, and curtains, and there is a massive TV over a *working* fireplace. And that TV? It has every channel known to man. Just to put this in perspective, the apartment I shared with Sam, Max, Mike, and Jenna could *fit* in Courtney's living room and the only TV was mine, in my *shared* room, where we would all occasionally huddle together on my second-hand twin bed to watch a show.

This is to say nothing of the fact that Courtney also has a full kitchen with a bar and stools where you can eat your meals, an *en suite* guest bedroom (unheard of in my world) and her own master bedroom suite which has a full bathroom, walk-in closet, fluffy cream-colored carpet, and sitting area with a desk, sofa, and second TV.

I knew my wife came from money.

I just didn't realize how much she had.

I didn't know she lived like this.

And I hate to say it, but it makes me a little bit uncomfortable.

I don't feel like this is my home, or even *our* home. It's *hers*, and there are no if, ands, or buts about it.

To be clear, my discomfort is not her fault. She's been nothing but welcoming to me. I went out to grab us sandwiches on Saturday afternoon and when I came back, she'd taken down a piece of expensive artwork that hung over the sofa in the living room and replaced it with my electric guitar. She unpacked my toiletries and placed them next to hers in the master bathroom. She insisted that I move the empty bureau from the guest room into the master bedroom for my clothes, and she cleared out her "off season" clothes to the guest room closet so that I could have half of the master closet. She told me to add whatever I want to the grocery list on the fridge and handed me the remote control to the TV when we sat down to eat our sandwiches.

Like I said, she's done everything she can to welcome me.

But I still feel like I'm visiting.

It just doesn't feel like home.

With one caveat:

In bed.

When it's just me and Courtney naked under the covers? It feels like *our* space, *our* place, *our* marriage. It feels like we're back in Scotland on the same soft, expensive, sweet-smelling sheets they had at our bed and breakfast. And when she's loud and lusty, crying out my name when I wring her pleasure? Fuck, yeah. I feel at home. I feel like the master of my new master bedroom.

It's just too bad we can't live in bed.

Or, you know, sleep in the same damn country.

On Monday morning, she kissed me goodbye while it was still dark out and left for Newark Airport en route to Tokyo, and she's coming back tonight. And tonight's Thursday night, which is also my first night back at work since I left to get married in June.

I probably should have told Courtney that I'd been in touch with Lulu and decided to go back to bartending at Tidewaters, but our texts have been so hot and/or tender over the last three days, I didn't want to rock the boat. She's landing soon. I'm heading to work at four and she's getting in at five. I figured I'd leave a note on the bed to come and find me at work. But now that I'm sitting here trying to write it, nothing is working for me.

Hey, Courts:

I'm at work.

Come and see me.
Josh

"Grrr." Nope. Too casual.

Babe,
I'm at work.
Come and find me.
I'll have a gimlet waiting.
J

Nope. Not quite right. It doesn't tell her how much I've missed her.

And I have *really* missed her, living all alone in this weird apartment-hotel hybrid over the last three days. I've missed sleeping with her, of course, but I've missed her laugh and her weird, out-of-nowhere factoids. I've missed her sleeping sounds and the smell of her shampoo when she washes her hair. I've missed ordering take-out together and watching TV on her couch. It's the longest we've been apart since our wedding, and I didn't like it one bit.

That said, though, I've gotten a lot done in this pristine, quiet space. In fact, I think the revisions to *Miss Gibson Will See You Now* are solid enough for me to submit my play to Simi Frederick's Emerging Playwrights competition, taking place this October in Boston. If it somehow manages to win first place, it'll be staged at Lincoln Center next February. And man, that would be a dream come true.

Frankly, I *should* be doing these revisions at the New Dramatists, but since I'm in "Avoid-Sam" mode, staying here felt safer. I haven't reached out to my ex since we got back to New York, and—*thank God*—she hasn't texted again. I'm not dumb enough to believe that she'll let it go, but I really don't want to deal with the confrontation if there's an option to ignore it. And I'm positive she's logging lots of hours at ND, waiting for me to show my face. No, thanks.

Speaking of confrontations I'd just as soon avoid, Courtney and I are spending next weekend—Fourth of July weekend—out in Greenwich with her parents, and I honestly believe a root canal sounds more appealing. Her parents have refused to take her calls and would only accept her offer to visit via e-mail. They're furious and looking for a pound of flesh, but they'd better not try to take it from her. I'll do whatever it takes to protect my wife and keep her safe, from her parents or anyone else.

Suddenly inspiration hits me, and my fingers fly across the keys:

To my wife,

I should have told you I decided to go back to work, but I didn't want to upset you. Don't be pissed. I need to make money.

Here's what you need to know right now:

1. I missed you, Court. I've missed you so goddamned much, it aches.

2. Come and find me at work, okay? I'll have a gimlet waiting.

3. Whether you show up or not, after work I'm coming home to you.

--Your Husband

I press the print icon and the note prints out on expensive, snow white paper, which I fold in half and prop on her pillow.

Then I change into a navy-blue Tidewaters T-shirt and my favorite jeans before grabbing the spare keys Courtney gave me and heading to work.

***

Courtney

All I want to do is order take-out, sink into a hot bath, curl up on the couch, and—if I can stay awake despite the jet-lag—make love to my husband before passing out.

The *last* thing I want to do is share a town car from Newark, New Jersey, back to Manhattan with my handsy boss, Joel Morris. Especially because Friday night traffic is making an early appearance on Thursday night and it's been stop 'n go on the Garden State since we were picked up at Terminal B.

I glance to my left, where Joel, whom I still think of as "Mr. Morris," is grinning at something on his phone, and say a quick prayer that he'll stay occupied with his phone throughout the drive to New York.

A lifelong friend of my father's, I grew up with Mr. and Mrs. Morris' twin daughters, Francesca and Antoinette, who moved to California with their mother when the Morrises divorced in '94. Since then, Joel has been re-married twice—both times to women half his age. Right now, he's between wives, and unless I'm mistaken—and the knot in the pit of my stomach tells me I'm not—he's on the hunt for wife number four.

Choosing to forget that his daughters splashed in the kiddie pool with me as toddlers, Joel turns to me with a sparkle in his eye.

"Courtney, you've really grown up into a fine woman."

"Thank you, Joel."

"Beautiful. Smart. Sexy."

I hope he'll shut up if I don't answer, but no such luck.

"Have I told you how much I admired the way you handled Mr. Hashimoto?"

At least five times.

"It's a good deal for us. I'm glad everything worked out," I answer, angling my legs away from him and turning my gaze to the window.

I drop my eyes to my very bare left hand, which rests on the windowsill. I didn't tell Josh, but until we speak to my parents, and to spare them further embarrassment, I decided not to wear my engagement or wedding rings on this trip to keep the news from their friends, like Joel Morris.

Hating the way my fingers look without the bands, I dip my other hand into my purse and find them in one of the pockets. I rub and finger the cool metal, wishing I could take them out and put them on.

"Little Courtney, the ball buster," he says, chuckling. Out of the corner of my eye, I note that his knees have spread out even more, taking up more than half the seat and invading my leg room with his knee. "Little Courtney...the *ball* buster." He rubs his hands back and forth on his thighs. "I wonder what else Little Courtney can do with *balls*."

Taking a deep breath, I steam inside a little, well aware that such innuendo isn't appropriate, but also fully cognizant to the fact that one of the reasons I fit into the "boys' club" of Wall Street is that I generally don't draw attention to this sort of low-level harassment. I ignore it. I swallow my indignation. I swallow it because my job affords me an excellent salary, and because one day, when I've had enough, I'll quit and open my own business. But by my calculations, I need at least two more years of work experience in an established firm before I can actually make a successful go of it. And it wouldn't hurt to make partner first too.

Jerky Joel wants to talk about balls? Fine.

"I play a decent game of tennis," I say lightly, careful to keep the edge out of my voice.

"Oh-ho!" he says. "Tennis, eh? Great idea. I'm not half-bad myself. How about we arrange a match? And a little wager to make things interesting? Winner buys dinner for the loser?"

Which means I lose either way.

I laugh demurely, projecting an amusement I don't feel. "I'd love it. But my weekends are booked to the hilt."

"After work some evening?" he persists, his voice suggestive.

I turn to him and smile. "How about we play doubles instead? If I recall, your girls were aces on the court. Are they coming out east any time soon? Maybe my father could join us too. Fathers versus daughters?"

"Fat chance. Frannie's expecting and Andi's spending all my money planning a wedding." He pauses, catching his lower lip between his teeth in a gesture I'm sure he believes to be sexy. "What about *you*, Courtney? You're a mature, successful woman now. Any wedding bells in *your* future?"

Only in my recent past, I think, remembering the shock of seeing Josh's face at the altar in Scotland almost two weeks ago. I move my fingers from my rings to my phone and pull it from my purse. It's almost six-thirty. I consider texting Josh that I'm stuck in traffic, but if our conversation should get as hot as the previous few, I wouldn't feel comfortable sitting here next to Joel while I'm sexting my husband.

Last night before I went to sleep in my luxury hotel room, we texted for about an hour, and by the end I was writhing against the sheets, doing everything he told me to do, everything to myself that he said he wished he was doing to me. And then finally, when neither of us could stand it anymore, we let go together, bringing ourselves to climax and promising that we'd do it again in person as soon as I got home.

Sighing with annoyance, I tuck my phone back into my bag and sit up straighter, crossing my arms over my chest.

Mistake.

My elbow is now close enough to Joel that he feels compelled to reach out to touch me with one stubby finger. He runs it slowly over my bare skin, making it crawl.

"You didn't answer my question," he murmurs.

I clear my throat. "I'm sorry?"

"I said you were beautiful. I asked if there were any wedding bells in your future."

Uncrossing my arms and pulling them inward, I reach into my bag for antibacterial gel. I squirt a small amount on my hands and then run them up my arms, paying special attention to the place where he was touching me. Stupid, sexist banter is one thing, but Joel Morris has no right—no *fucking* right—to lay a finger on me without my permission.

"Maybe," I say, my voice unmistakably cool, because I've had enough. "In fact, I'm quite serious about someone right now."

"You're seeing someone?" His bushy, gray eyebrows furrow. "Since when? Who?"

"We attended the Frederick wedding together last month."

He blusters with annoyance. "Someone I know?"

"I don't think so. He's a playwright. From Minnesota."

"A-A *playwright?*" he sputters. "From *Minnesota?*" His face quickly segues from annoyance to amusement and he chortles loudly. "Ha! You're kidding."

"I'm not," I assure him. "If there *are* any wedding bells in my future, Joel, it'll be because of him."

"Huh. Your father'll have something to say about that. Wasting your life on a playwright. An *artist*," he snipes, hissing it like it's a bad word. "My Frannie's a smart girl. She married a trader."

"Good for Frannie."

"And Andi's marrying a tech *genius.*"

I tap my chin. "Is this her second time down the aisle? Or third?"

"Second," he huffs, picking up his phone and—*thank God*—angling his body away from mine.

As I stare out my window, watching our slow progress through the Lincoln Tunnel, however, I regret losing my cool. One doesn't get ahead on Wall Street by making rich old men feel like impotent fools.

For a second, I consider trying to smooth things over with a little flirtation or a joke about playwrights, but I can't bring myself to do it. I don't want to. I don't want to kiss Joel Morris' fat ass, and I don't want to sell out Josh to do it. Card played, card laid. I just hope he stops making these awful come-ons once we're back at the office, because it's gross and I'm so goddamned sick of it.

My phone buzzes and I pull it out.

Where are you?

I can't help the wave of happiness that sweeps over me. Three words. A dozen characters. And I'm undone.

I run the pad of my finger lightly over the letters, feeling warmth spread throughout my body. Neither of us has used the word "love" yet, but more and more, I wonder if love is what I'm feeling. What else but love could summon such a wellspring of joy from twelve letters arranged just so?

Traffic, I type. *Should be there soon.*

I've missed you, baby, he answers.

Butterflies.

In my stomach. In my chest. Flitting everywhere inside of me and causing ripples of pleasure wherever they land.

I've missed you too.

I stare at the screen, waiting for more.

See you soon?

We emerge from the tunnel onto the streets of New York and the hustle of the city on a summer evening surrounds us. Young couples walk hand in hand to restaurants. A mother pushes a jogging-stroller holding a giggling toddler. Two handsome men walk side by side, drinking iced coffees.

Really soon, I write back.

When the car pulls up in front of my building, I turn to Joel, that feeling of wanting to smooth things over almost overwhelming.

"Well," I say, "this is me."

He turns his head slowly and looks at me with a bored expression. Shit. He's still stewing.

"I'm so glad it was a successful venture," I add. "Thanks for your trust in me."

"Mmm."

"I'm looking forward to working with more of our international offices."

He stares back at me, his eyes narrowing a little. "We'll see."

If he's trying to set me off-balance, it's working, and I *hate it* that it's working. Maybe I took it too far with the sanitizing gel maneuver?

"See you tomorrow?" I ask, my voice airy and small.

"I suppose." He shrugs. "We work at the same office, don't we?"

Oh, for the love—

"We do." I open my door and toss over my shoulder, "Good night, Joel. Get home safely."

Without saying goodbye, he turns away from me, so I slam the door shut and get ten dollars out of my purse to tip the driver, who's already put my bag on the curb.

As the car pulls away, I tell myself that Joel Morris is a

spoiled baby, pitching a mini-fit because he didn't get his way. Well, screw that. I have a hot husband waiting for me upstairs. I don't need—or want—to spend any more time on Joel—fucking—Morris tonight.

I wave to the doorman and step onto the elevator, trying to let go of the stress of the past three and a half days and focusing my attention on the man waiting for me upstairs. He's all that matters now. Josh. My Josh. My husband. My sanctuary.

I can't unlock the door fast enough, flinging it open so hard that it bangs into the foyer wall.

"Josh?" I call. "I'm home!"

Leaving my bags in the front hall, I kick off my shoes and hurry toward the living room.

"Miss me?" I ask as I round the corner.

But the room is dim and quiet, like no one's been here for a while.

"Josh?" I glance over my shoulder at the kitchen as I head down the back hall to our room. Maybe he's—*oh my God! Yes!*—waiting in bed for me?

But when I open the bedroom door, it's as still as the living room. Confused, I look around the room for any hint of where he might be, and my eyes land on a note folded atop my pillow.

Hurrying over to the bed, I pick it up and read it, then plop down on the side of the bed, blinking back the tears of intense disappointment that instantly well up in my eyes.

He's not here. He's at...work.

I scan the note again, then take a deep breath, closing

my eyes as I lie back on the bed.

All I wanted was to spend one-on-one time with my husband tonight. Maybe take a hot bath together and curl up in the big spoon of his body as we watched TV in our bed. The *last* thing I want to do after a twelve-hour flight from Tokyo, is go to Tidewaters and watch him get hit on by women younger, thinner, and prettier than me.

"Why, Josh?" I mutter, sitting up and placing the note on the bedside table. "Why didn't you tell me?"

It hurts that he didn't discuss any of this with me. As I wander back toward the foyer to grab my phone, I wonder when he decided to go back to work. I thought that marriage meant making these sorts of big decisions together.

I take my phone out of my purse and text: *Hey. I'm home. I thought you would be too.*

While I'm walking into the kitchen to pour myself a glass of water, my phone vibrates. *Did you get my note?*

I take a long sip of water and then write back: *Yes. But I didn't know you were working tonight. I didn't realize you were still working at Tidewaters.*

He answers quickly: *I told you I needed to make money.*

And I told you I'd cover our bills, I type.

That doesn't work for me, baby.

"Nor does you flirting with a bunch of single, hot women work for me, Josh!" I say aloud, finishing the water and putting the glass in the sink.

Court, come and see me. I missed you so much.

I missed him too, but I feel like a mess. I'm tired. I'm jet-lagged. I smell like a plane, my ankles are swollen, my hair is greasy, I need to unpack and—and all I want to do is cry. I hate it that he's not here. I hate it that he didn't talk to me about going back to work.

And, maybe more than anything else, I hate it that I'm so fucking insecure.

Not in the mood, I type. *I'll see you when you get home.*

Stop pouting, he replies. *I made you a gimlet. It's waiting.*

For a second, I consider going. I really do. But I don't have the energy it would take to get ready and look halfway decent. Pulling my roller-bag into the bedroom, I sink down onto the bed.

Long flight. I'm really tired. I'm going to take a bath and get into bed. See you later.

I stare at the phone, willing him to write back, but he doesn't. After ten minutes of waiting, I wipe away my tears of self-pity and glumly go draw myself a bath.

***

Josh

When she wrote back that she was taking a bath and going to bed, I almost left my shift to go talk to her. To talk *some sense* into her.

Yeah, I was also rolling my eyes.

And yeah, part of me was pissed that she was guilt-tripping me for going back to work.

But mostly, it was making me crazy that after four days apart, she was so close and I couldn't have my hands on her body, my lips on her skin.

When it came time to take my break at ten, I considered

it again—running home to see her real quick—but once we were together again, I had no idea how I'd force myself to return to work, so I told myself to wait to go home until my shift was over.

And that's when I realized something. For the first time since moving in with Courtney last weekend, I thought of her apartment as "home." Why, I wondered, would I suddenly use that word about a place where I so clearly didn't belong? Where I didn't feel "at home" just a few hours before?

That's when something amazing occurred to me: that Courtney was at the apartment now. That was the only major difference…which made me realize that wherever Courtney was, *that* place was my home. Even if she was pouting and pissed and mad at me, wherever she was, was the only place I wanted to be.

The last three hours of my shift flew by after that.

As I unlock the door and step into the dark, quiet apartment at ten after one, I appreciate the fact that I am *home*; that this place, with its fancy decorations and chair rail molding and spare bedroom, is where I *live*, where my heart wants to be. I savor the knowledge that the woman I married almost two weeks ago is sleeping a few feet away from where I'm standing, and in a matter of seconds, she'll be in my arms.

I don't care if she's mad at me. Truth be told, I'm a little mad at her too.

I throw my keys on the foyer table and make my way through the dimly-lit hallway. There's no sign of my wife in the kitchen or living room. Turning right, I step into the back hallway and gingerly open the door to our bedroom.

In the moonlight, I can see her face, pale and relaxed, like Snow White before Prince Charming's kiss. I pause for a second, watching her chest rise and fall under the covers, taking in her still-damp hair that she must have washed in the tub. I can smell honeysuckle, oh-so-lightly, and I breathe it in deeply because it's Courtney's smell and I'm so fucking glad she's finally home.

Shutting the door behind me, I reach behind my neck and pull off my T-shirt. My jeans and boxers come next, littering the floor. I head into the bathroom to wash off eight hours of spilled drinks and sweat, my cock hardening as I think about every dirty thing I want to do to my wife once I slip into bed, naked and hungry, beside her.

I towel off and turn off the bathroom light, stepping into our bedroom.

As my eyesight adjusts to the darkness, I realize that Courtney's awake. She's lying on her side with her cheek on the pillow, facing the bathroom, eyes open.

"Hi," she says, her voice small and soft.

"Hi," I whisper, leaning against the bathroom doorway.

"Why didn't you tell me?"

"What?"

"That you'd decided to go back to work."

"I knew you wouldn't like it."

"So…so you just didn't *tell* me? You just…did it?"

She sniffles, and I wonder if she's been crying. I really don't like the thought that my actions have hurt her, but she's not my ruler, she's my partner. And if we don't establish equity in the beginning of our marriage, I'll only have myself to blame when she feels she can call all the shots.

"I told you it was important to me."

"You still should have told me."

She's right. I should have.

"Maybe so," I concede, "but I didn't want to fight with you, Court."

"Well…you have to," she says.

"I…*have* to?" I ask, still standing buck naked by the bathroom.

"Yes!" she exclaims, sitting up and giving me a prepared speech. "I'm not going to like a lot of stuff you do. And—and maybe you're not going to like a lot of stuff I do. But that doesn't mean we keep it from each other. We still have to *talk* about it."

"Okay," I say, walking over to the bed. She shimmies over a little and I sit down, twisting my body a little to face her. "Then let's talk about it."

"You don't have to work," she says.

"Yes," I answer. "I do."

"No! You don—"

"Baby, I need you to stop doing that, okay? I don't *want* you to support me. I don't *need* you to support me. It's awesome that you make a lot of money, but I want to contribute too. I can work on my plays and bartend at the same time. I *like* working. I *like* Tidewaters—"

"Why?" she demands, her voice a little crazier than it

was a second ago.

"What?"

"Why do you like it so much?"

"Well…Lulu's been good to me. She's really flexible with my hours and she pays an above-average hourly rate. I make good money in tips. Not to mention, it's walkable from our apartment, and it's—"

"Full of beautiful women!" she cries.

"What?" I blink at her, totally taken aback by this outburst.

She looks utterly miserable, clasping her hands in her lap. For the first time, I realize she's not wearing her rings, and I feel a stone cold settle in the pit of my stomach.

"Where are your rings?"

"Oh," she murmurs. "They're in my purse."

"Why aren't you wearing them?"

She swipes at the tears sliding down her cheeks. "Because my boss is a friend of my father's and my parents are so angry, and I didn't want to add fuel to the fire by—by—"

"I get it," I say, even though I don't like the sight of her bare fingers. "Can we go back to the part about there being beautiful women at Tidewaters, which, personally, I find a debatable point?"

"Not debatable," she says, sniffling. "I go there a lot. I see them. They're hot."

"Totally debatable to *me*," I say, reaching for her face and cupping her cheek. I use my thumb to swipe away a fat tear. "It *wasn't* full of beautiful women tonight. The *most* beautiful woman in the whole world didn't show. She took a bath and went to bed."

"I'm not—"

"Shut up," I tell her, leaning forward to press my lips to her forehead. "To me, you are."

"Josh," she whispers, her voice breaking on my name.

My lips brush her skin when I ask, "Is that what this has been about? All of your objections to me working? You're worried about the women who come into the bar?"

She nods against me, sniffling again. "They all f-flirt with you. They all...I mean, I used to b-be one of them, J-Josh. They all w-want you and I'm j-just—"

I cradle her face in my hands. "Baby, look at me."

Her cheeks glisten from tears, and I know she's upset, but the fact that she's upset because she feels possessive of me somehow makes it okay that she didn't have her rings on. It balances things out. Maybe it doesn't make perfect sense...but sorting out feelings as a newlywed is a damned uneven science.

"You're my *wife*, Court. You *belong* to me," I say. "And I belong to you. *To you.* No one else. It doesn't matter how many women check me out or ask for my phone number or overtip me, hoping to get into my pants. It doesn't matter if a parade of supermodels walks in, or the Dallas Cowboy cheerleading squad, or if the Sirens leave their rocks in the sea and make an appearance at my bar. I'm not going to care. I'm not available. There is only one thing that matters to me."

Her expression, so earnest, makes my heart swell.

"What?"

"You. You and me. Us. Nobody else." I scan her eyes. "Courtney Jane Salinger, there is only you for me."

"Dalton," she murmurs, her eyes flicking to my lips. "Courtney Jane...*Dalton*."

Because my name on her tongue is so fucking sexy, and I can't wait anymore to touch her, I lean forward and press my mouth to hers. She opens for me like a flower, her lips tasting of sleep and salt. Her skin is warm and smells like fresh sheets and honeysuckle after the rain. I lean her back against the pillows and roll on top of her, annoyed by the comforter between us. But I cup her face and kiss her senselessly, letting her know that she's the only woman in my life, the only woman I want.

"You have nothing to worry about," I say. "I promise."

I'm not sure she believes me, but she smiles at me as she wipes away the last of her tears, and I feel relieved. I roll off of her and reach for the comforter, to draw it back and join her under the covers, but she stops me, pointing at her bureau.

"My purse is over there. Grab it for me?"

I cross the room quickly to retrieve her bag and place it on the bed beside her. She reaches into an inside pocket and pulls out her engagement and wedding rings, opening her palm to show them to me.

"I'm sorry I took them off," she says. "I didn't want to. I missed wearing them."

"I understand," I say, plucking them from her hand and fitting them, one at a time, back onto the fourth finger of her left hand. Dropping my lips to her fingers, I kiss them tenderly before gazing up at her. "Back where they belong. You *and* them."

"I…Josh, I… I think maybe I…" She swallows so hard, I swear I can hear it, but then she presses her lips together, blinking at me in the moonlight. After a second, she says, "I missed you so much."

Something in the back of my mind wonders if telling me she missed me was her original intent, and it thrills me for a second that she even considered saying something else. So much, in fact, that when I slip under the covers beside her, I am determined to show her—in every possible way— how much I missed her too.

CHAPTER 3

• IN-LAWS •

"Building boundaries with in-laws early in your marriage is imperative, and much easier than undoing early patterns of intrusive or divisive behavior later on."

--Dr. Sydney Morningstar

<u>Courtney</u>

The last time Josh and I took the train out to Connecticut to visit with my parents, we were sitting across from each other, dressed to the nines, heading to a posh, country club wedding. It was also the first time we held hands, and the first time we ever danced together.

After that night, I couldn't deny my feelings for Josh any longer. I knew I was falling for him, I just didn't know how to marry my yearning to be matched with my growing feelings for the neighborhood bartender who, by the way, had already friend-zoned me.

Looking back now, I couldn't have possibly predicted what would end up happening.

He followed me to England and married me.

So, this time we're sitting side by side on the train.

And the man I fell for while dancing in the moonlight is now my husband.

"So," he asks, taking my hand as the train pulls away from Grand Central Station, "on a scale from one to ten, how painful will this weekend be?"

"Eleventy-eight," I say, looking up at him with a half-grimace, half-grin.

"That bad?"

"They're not happy."

"Why do you think Lucy told them?"

I sigh. "She loves my dad. He's her only sibling. In their own way, they're close. I don't think she was comfortable keeping our news from him *before* the ceremony, but she did...out of love for me. After it was done? I think she felt compelled to tell him. Especially because it was too late for him to try and stop me."

He nods. "We need to tell my parents too. Sooner than later."

I know that Josh talks to his family after church every Sunday. I've overheard him chatting with them the past few weekends. I don't know if he realizes that he slips into a pronounced midwestern accent during their conversations together, but he does, and I find it completely charming.

"Will they be upset?" I ask.

He gives me a look.

"Of course they will." I answer my own question, then shift in my seat a little to face him better. Recalling his earlier question, I ask, "On a scale from one to ten, how painful will it be?"

He looks sad, his brows furrowing for just a second before he drops my hand and rubs his jaw. "They'll be hurt."

"Hurt." My shoulders droop. "Ugh. I think that's worse than mad."

"My parents are going to love you," he assures me, "but they're old-fashioned. Certain things are supposed to be done certain ways in their world. If I was serious about someone, they would've expected to meet her and celebrate at least one holiday together while we were still dating. Bringing you home for a holiday would have been a big deal. And then, once we were engaged, they'd expect us to come back for an engagement celebration." He pauses, a slight smile on his face. "My mom would've wanted to help out with the wedding. Not a lot. She wouldn't try to take over or anything. But, you know, she would have offered to make little favors. Or arrange the flowers. Or choose a favorite prayer to read during the ceremony."

"Your parents are pretty religious, huh?"

He nods. "Yeah. Church every Sunday. Fellowship coffee and bible study after. Kitchen cleaning crew on Monday nights. Bingo on Tuesdays. Fellowship dinner on Wednesdays. Youth group on Fridays. We practically lived at church. It was a big part of my childhood."

"What about *you*?" I ask, realizing that I know nothing about my husband's faith or belief system.

"What *about* me?"

Part of me is uncomfortable asking about Josh's religion, like it's something too personal to pick at or ask about. This is the challenge of our marriage, though. Things we would have learned about one another dating organically are now mysteries to be discovered within the framework of marriage.

"Are you religious?" I ask. "Do you go to church? I don't even know."

"I'm not a zealot, but yeah, I belong to a church."

"Wait. You do? Here, in New York?"

He nods. "Gustavus Adolphus Lutheran. It's on East 22nd."

I'm surprised. I mean, I go to church with my parents on Christmas Eve and Easter morning if I am spending the holidays out in Connecticut, but I don't know anyone my age who goes to church with any regularity, let alone claims membership as an independent adult.

"You're serious?" I ask.

He lifts his chin a little and his eyes, which have been warm and open during our conversation thus far, narrow just a little. "I joined when I moved here eight years ago."

I stare at him. "And you go. On Sundays. Regularly."

"It's hard sometimes, but yeah, I try to get there once a month."

"And you *believe* all of that stuff?"

"Stuff?"

"About God and Jesus and the Virgin Mary and the wine being his blood and the bread being his skin and—"

"Skin?" He cringes at me. "Court, what are you talking about?"

"You know what I mean…flesh. Body. The bread is the body, right?"

"Lutherans don't believe that communion bread *becomes* the body of Christ, but we do believe that the bread and wine co-exist in communion with—"

"Oh my God. You really believe it all. Like, *really*."

"Yeah," he says, nodding at me. "I believe it all. Like, *really*."

I'm staring at this man, *my husband*, in a whole new light, trying to reconcile the man I know with one who believes in religious hocus-pocus. I don't believe that virgins can give birth, or that wine suddenly becomes blood because a priest blesses it. That's just nonsense, isn't it? Honestly, I regard most biblical stories as closer to fairytales than actual history. While I think religion can imbue holidays with a certain charm and cultural *gravitas*, and I think it's important to be a good person, I don't actually *believe* in the nuts and bolts of Christianity. And it turns out I'm married to someone who *does*.

"You're *religious*," I whisper.

"You say it like it's a *bad* thing," he whispers back.

"It's definitely a *surprising* thing. A lot of it defies logic, don't you think?"

"Or requires faith." He crosses his arms over his chest and sighs. "I don't shove it down anyone else's throat. Frankly, I think faith and belief are pretty personal. Yes, I believe in God. Yes, I believe that Jesus was his son on earth. Yes, I take communion on Sundays when I manage to get to church. But, it's *my* thing, Courtney; you don't have to believe in any of it. You don't have to go with me."

"I don't mind going to church services," I say. This is the truth. I find church services, with their soothing prayers and familiar hymns, comforting. And like Josh, I think faith and belief are personal. As long as someone else's beliefs aren't pushed on me, I maintain a "live and let live"-style philosophy on organized religion. "I just...I had no idea *you* were so...you know...church-y."

"I'm not *"church-y,"* whatever the hell that is. I'm not from another planet just because I believe in God, Courtney."

"Of course not. I didn't say that."

"Then stop looking at me like I'm about to bust out the catechism."

"I don't even know what that is."

"And like I said, you don't have to go with me," he says. "I mean, I wouldn't even ask that—"

"Would you want our kids to go?"

I swear, I had no idea I was going to ask that question. I have no clue where it came from, but I quickly remember the last time Josh and I discussed having children. It was the day after our wedding, and Josh essentially freaked out, telling me he wasn't even sure he wants kids.

He stares at me hard, then says, "That's not a relevant question, Courtney."

He's right. It's not. We don't have kids and we might never have them, a fact that makes a sadness so sharp and real stab at my heart, I force myself not to dwell on it, not to give it purchase.

"I'd like to go with you sometime," I blurt out, moving the conversation back to a safer place. "I'd like to check out your church."

"You don't have to."

"I want to."

The tension in his body seems to ease and I feel relieved.

"Well, you're welcome to come with me anytime," he says. "It'll be easier to go… now that Lulu took me off weekends."

"Wait! What?"

I can't help the burst of happiness inside of me. Since our late-night discussion two weeks ago when Josh first went back to work, I've been careful to project neutrality about him working, even though I have lingering unease. I don't have any right to try to control him, and as long as he swears that I'm the only woman in his life, I have to trust that whatever temptations lurk at Tidewaters, my husband will resist them.

That said, this news is welcome and wonderful. No more Friday nights at the meat market.

"Yep. She changed my hours."

"To what?"

He grins at me, taking my hand in his and kissing my knuckles. "I didn't like it that you were working Monday to Friday and I was working Thursday, Friday, and Sunday. It meant we didn't have any time together except Saturdays, and that didn't feel like enough. So I talked to Lulu and she changed some things around. Now I'm working Monday through Thursday, every night from four to midnight. Weekends off."

I drop his hand and throw my arms around his neck, arching my back so that my chest presses into his. "Thank you."

"Compromise, right?" he asks, surprised laughter making his voice extra-warm.

"And less hotties to hit on you," I say, leaning back to look at his face.

"Only hottie I want is right here."

I lean forward and press my lips to his, moaning softly when he swipes his tongue against mine and pulls me closer. We kiss for a few seconds before I realize that an older woman across the aisle is clearing her throat loudly.

When I peek at her over Josh's shoulder, she says, "Get a room, huh? There's kids here."

I lean back to look at Josh and we both giggle, naughty kids caught necking on the train.

"So…" I clear my throat. "Um…back to…um, your parents."

"Your face is beet red," he teases.

"It's hot in here."

He chuckles again, kissing the tip of my nose.

"My parents. Yeah. My parents will be hurt." He pauses for a second, then asks, "Hey…How would you feel about spending Thanksgiving with them? We could go out to Minnesota on Wednesday and come back on Sunday? I think it would really help to smooth things over."

Hmm. My first instinct is to say no. My parents do an *amazing* Thanksgiving dinner at their house in Greenwich, and the day after, we go to town for caroling, hot cocoa, and the annual Greenwich Christmas tree lighting. It's one of my favorite annual traditions and I really hate to miss it, but...*compromises*. Marriage means compromise.

"Sure," I say. "That sounds great. We can look at flights when we get home."

He grins at me, looking relieved. "Awesome. I'm planning to tell them about us on Sunday. Maybe you could get on the phone too? Chat with my mom for a few minutes?"

"Of course. Sure."

"She'll like you," he says, though his lingering look at my face conveys hope, not certainty.

I smile at him, thinking about this woman who gave birth to Josh, who loved him first—about how she took him to church four times a week and drove him back and forth to school. She would have wiped his sniffles and put Band-Aids on his scraped knees. I don't know what she'll think of me, and we certainly come from very different places, but I'm determined to like her, to find some common ground where we can exist together.

"Now back to *your* parents," says Josh, taking my hand again and lacing his fingers through mine. "Do you think they've got anything planned for this weekend? Or will we sit in high back chairs all weekend staring each other down?"

"Oh, that sounds like a super good time...but sadly, no. The high back Inquisition chairs are on loan to the Met. We'll have to settle for a clambake and fireworks at the yacht club instead."

"Do you really have chairs from the Inquisition?"

"Don't be stupid."

"Your parents are stupid rich, Court. Anything's

possible."

"They have a couple of Renoirs, a Picasso, and a Monet. They collect paintings, not chairs."

"Originals?"

"Of course."

Josh chuckles. "Of course."

"Are you nervous?"

"Not of your parents." He caresses my cheek with his free hand. "I won't let them hurt you, baby. I promise."

His words touch me. I know that Josh has a protective streak when it comes to me—hell, he crossed an ocean to be sure I didn't marry the wrong guy—but it makes my heart squeeze a little to know I'm not facing my father's wrath all alone.

"It'll be fine. They're just angry."

"Anger's okay," he says. "Disrespect isn't." He takes a deep breath and sighs. "Any idea what to expect?"

"My mother will cry," I say, "but it'll be more for show. She isn't sad she missed our wedding; she's just sad that she missed out on the opportunity to throw a massive party and show off their money. My father's a different story. He's good and pissed. He'll bluster about my irresponsibility and my duty to my family and yell about elopements being trashy and—"

"That's not going to work for me," says Josh, his expression severe. "Your mom's tears I can handle. I'm sure my mother will cry a little too. But "trashy"? I'm not comfortable with anyone throwing that word around about me...or my wife."

Part of me is thrilled by what Josh is saying; that he won't allow anyone—even my parents—speak badly of me in his presence. But the reality is that I've always let my father scream and shout and clench his fists at the sky when he's pissed, because after he's gotten all of that out of his system, he's much more manageable. Might he call me names? Sure. Might he call Josh's and my marriage a "sham" or the way we went about getting married "shameful"? He might. But it's better just to let him rage a while. It's the way I've always done things.

"He doesn't really mean it," I say.

"That doesn't make it okay."

"I know," I say, using a pacifying voice. "But honestly, it'll be better if you just let him say his piece. He'll get everything off his chest and then we can talk."

"As long as "getting everything off his chest" means that he's disapproving, but respectful, it'll be fine."

"Well, just to calibrate your expectations appropriately, he might not initially be...*respectful*," I say, "but it's really best to just let him—"

"Courtney," says Josh, an edge creeping into his voice, "I hear what you're saying. I really do, babe. You're telling me to let him say whatever he wants to us and take it, and then, when he's done insulting us every which way he can think of, we can all speak reasonably."

I nod, relieved that he understands how we do things at Chez Salinger. "Exactly. Just...tune him out, and when he's done, we'll all move on."

"Baby, I can't do that," he says softly.

"I know you want to stick up for me," I say, starting to feel the slightest bit frustrated. These are my parents, after all, and I think I know the best way to deal with them. "And that means the world to me, Josh. It really does, but this is my father, and—"

"And if he can't speak respectfully to his daughter, *my wife*, we're leaving."

"No, we're not," I tell him. "We're not just leaving. We're letting him do his thing, and then we'll talk. I don't care if he gets mad. He has a right to be mad. He'll be mad. We'll listen. He'll calm down and it'll all be okay."

"I agree he has a right to be mad. But he doesn't have the right to call you trash, or—"

"They're just words! He doesn't *mean* them."

"That's the second time you've said that, and it sounds a lot like enabling."

What the hell? My mouth drops open. "*Enabling*?"

"If he doesn't mean them, he shouldn't say them…and you shouldn't let him."

"I don't *let* him! It's just easier."

"Easier isn't better, Courtney."

"Get off your high horse, *Josh*. Just because I deal with things differently in my family than you do in yours doesn't make our way wrong."

"Name calling is wrong, no matter how you slice it. Not to mention, you're not just you anymore. You're half of a couple, that includes me, and either we, as a unit, deserve and demand respect from our families, or we don't. Which is it?"

"Not everything is so black and white!" I say, unlacing my fingers from his and crossing my arms over my chest.

"This is," he says, his voice soft, but firm.

"So, what's the plan?" I demand. "The second my father starts shouting, we walk out?"

"No," says Josh. "I will calmly and politely ask him to stop shouting and to refrain from any insulting language. If he can speak reasonably to us, we can all have a great conversation."

I blink at him, then shake my head with exasperation. "Oh, that's a great plan. William Salinger *loves it* when young, broke playwrights tell him what he can and cannot say and do in his own home. That'll go over like gangbusters. Awesome. You've got it all figured out."

"Back up," he says, his eyes narrowing at me for the second time on this goddamned train ride from hell. "What does it matter if I'm a playwright?"

Shit!

"What?" I ask, stalling for time.

Shit, shit, shit.

Up to now, I've never told Josh that my father's opinion of the arts is that its pursuit should remain firmly in the milieu of hobby or patron with no exceptions and no in-between.

"Your dad doesn't respect the fact that I'm a playwright, does he?"

Fuck. I don't know how to say this, because no, my father does not and will not respect Josh's chosen profession, even on the day he's at the tippy-top of it.

"Courtney?"

"He's…oh, Josh. Come on…" I groan. "Fine. The truth? He probably would have preferred it if you were a lawyer or doctor or something."

"Oh. Okay," he says slowly, a bitterness I've never heard before stealing the usual warmth of his voice. "I see. So, not only did I elope with his daughter, but I'm not good enough for her in the first place, am I?"

"I didn't say that."

"Yeah," he says, angling his whole body toward the window. "You did."

"Josh," I murmur, putting my hand on his arm. "Please. *I* don't think that. You know I don't think that. I love it that you're a playwright. I believe in you."

He sighs, still angled toward the window, his attention focused on the changing landscape outside the train as we zoom into Connecticut.

"Josh?" I say, hating that this is so hard and wishing that everything could be easier.

"Either we're a team or we're not," he says, turning to look at me, his eyes hurt which makes me want to cry. "Which is it?"

***

Josh

My wife's eyes have filled with tears, and I fucking hate to see them, but I also can't let them derail us. We're two stops away from Old Greenwich and I need for us to be on the same page when we get there.

I don't give a shit what was considered "normal" at the Salinger house before now—no, that's not true. I care. It just wasn't my personal business—but no man, no matter who he is, has the right to treat my wife with disrespect. And if I allow it in my presence? In hers? I'm no better than him. If I don't object, I'm allowing it, and I can't do that. I won't.

"We're a team," she says softly.

"Baby," I say, pulling her against me, "I care about you. I care about us. And if we let anyone—your father included—treat us like crap, what does that say about us? It says that we're okay with people shitting on our marriage, shitting on us. Well, I'm not. We might have gone about things in an unconventional way, but we made our vows in front of God, and they're real to me."

"They're real to me too," she says, looking up at me from within the circle of my arms, "but I just don't see why—"

"Because you're my wife."

"I'm also their daughter."

As the train rolls into Old Greenwich, I squeeze her a little tighter. "Let's just see how it goes, huh?"

"Okay," she murmurs, preceding me out of the train car as I grab our bags and follow her.

She walks to the left, toward a little station, raising her hand in greeting. Following the direction of the gesture, I see a black Mercedes sedan parked at the end of the ramp. An older man in a chauffeur cap exits the vehicle and waves back.

"Hello, Gordon!" calls Courtney.

"Good afternoon, Miss Courtney," he answers, nodding at her.

He pops the trunk for me, and I place our bags inside.

"I'm Josh, Courtney's husband."

"Mr. Dalton," he says in a clipped English accent. "Welcome to Connecticut."

"Thanks, Gordon."

"Gordon's been with our family since I was a little girl," says Courtney, her voice warm.

"May I offer my congratulations on your marriage, miss?"

"Thank you, yes."

He opens the back door for Courtney, but I'm not about to make him open mine. I slip inside as he slams her shut.

"What's with the "miss" stuff?" I whisper.

She hushes me as Gordon slides into the driver's seat and a moment later, we are driving to Courtney's parents' house.

The one time we were out in Connecticut together, we didn't visit her house, so I have no idea what to expect and only movies for a frame of reference. Suffice it to say, nothing prepares me for "Ulcombe Place," the 7,000-square foot, one hundred and twenty-year-old, six-bedroom mansion on Long Island Sound, where Courtney Jane Salinger grew up.

Gordon pulls up to a stone portico and puts the car in park, popping the trunk before opening Courtney's door. I take the bags from the trunk noting, for the first time, that my hands are sweating.

Fuck, of course they're sweating. This place is the size of a castle, I married the princess, and the king hates my guts. I think I'm allowed a little sweating.

No one welcomes us, but I remind myself that it's Courtney's house when she opens the thick, medieval-looking door and steps into the marble entryway.

"Mother?" she calls. "Father?"

No answer.

She turns to me with a weak smile. "You can put the bags wherever. Someone will take them up to my room."

"I'm perfectly capable of taking our bags—"

Her eyes widen with an implied warning. "Please."

With a sigh, I put the bags down beside an antique side table that holds a massive vase full of fresh flowers. To the left of the vase is a gilded mirror and my wife takes a moment to look at her reflection.

Because she looks so stressed and so unhappy, I move behind her and put my arms around her waist, resting my chin on her shoulder.

"You're beautiful," I say.

She takes a deep breath, staring at herself intently and lowering her chin like she's about to head into battle.

"And I'm crazy about you," I add, pressing a soft kiss behind her ear.

Her expression softens as her eyes meet mine. "You are?"

"I am," I say, realizing how much courage it must have taken for her to get married-at-first-sight, knowing all along that she'd eventually have to submit herself to this abuse.

"And I think you're very brave," I whisper, kissing her again.

"I'm not," she says, still holding my eyes in the mirror.

"Yes, you are," I assure her. "And a little nuts."

That makes her laugh and I think it's the first genuine smile I've seen since the train pulled into Greenwich.

"*I'm* nuts?"

"Uh-huh," I say, loving our reflection in the mirror. My arms are clasped under her full breasts, which is plumping them against the scoop neck of her light pink T-shirt. "You married a stranger."

"I married *you*," she says, placing her hands over mine.

"Like I said...nuts."

She giggles softly, leaning back into me as I run my lips down the column of her neck, from behind her ear to her collarbone.

"I'm crazy about you too," she whispers, sighing softly when I nuzzle her soft skin.

When I open my eyes, hers are waiting for me. "Remember that. No matter what happens today, remember that we're crazy about each other...and we might be nuts, but we're nuts together. We're a team, Court. Team Dalton."

"Team Dalton," she says, a heartbreaking smile taking over her face.

"You and me."

"You're awfully good with words," she says.

"Maybe I should do something about it."

"Like write plays," she suggests, grinning at me as she

leans her head to the side to give me better access to her delicious neck. "I bet you'd be great at it."

"Are you two *quite* finished?" booms a voice from several feet away.

We've been caught canoodling by Courtney's father, but to my surprise—and immense satisfaction—Courtney doesn't leap out of my arms like a scared rabbit. She reaches for my hand, lacing her fingers through mine. And that's how we approach her father: hand in hand. Unified.

Like I said, my girl is nuts and brave.

"Hello, father."

"CJ," he says with a curt nod.

"I believe you know my husband, Josh."

"Dalton," he says in acknowledgement, his lips pursing like he just sucked on a lime. He slides his eyes back to his daughter. "Your mother is upstairs in her room."

"Will she be joining us?"

"I have no idea. She's *very* upset."

I squeeze my wife's hand in solidarity.

"I'm sorry to hear that," Courtney answers, her voice level and strong.

"She's *very* disappointed in your choices, miss. As am I."

I take a deep breath, hold it, then let it go. I'm uncomfortable by his words and his tone, but he's not yelling and he's not speaking disrespectfully...yet.

"You have a right to be disappointed, father."

It's like her words flick a switch, and suddenly her father, who was managing to keep it together a moment before, snaps.

"Damn straight I do! Running off to London with this—this—*playwright*! If you think you're going to get a dime of my money, missy, you're out of your goddamned mind! Throwing your life away on—"

"That's enough," I growl, stepping forward.

"*You* won't tell me when enough is enough in my own goddamned house! Who do you think you are? You're *nothing*! You're some goddamned gold digger, probably trying to knock up my daughter so she's trapped with your brats for the rest of her goddamned life. Well, no sir! If you think I'm going to stand by and let that happen, you've got another goddamned thing coming to you..." He continues to yell, his face getting redder and redder by the second as his ugly words bounce off the hard marble and echo in my ears.

I'm fisting my free hand by my side, about five seconds away from throwing a punch at my wife's father, when Courtney shocks the hell out of me by turning her back on her father, and facing her whole body toward mine. Her eyes, which are somehow sparkling and severe at the same time, search mine.

"What was the plan again?" she asks. "...that we leave, right?"

As her father rages on behind her, I nod.

"Then get the bags. Let's go."

Without thinking, I turn around and pick up the two bags from beside the table.

"Well, father," she says, "this has been a delight, but we must run."

"Wh-What? What's this? I haven't said—"

"Yes, you have," she says. "You've said quite enough. You can't speak to my husband like this. And you can't speak to me like this anymore. When you're ready to—to speak to us, um, politely and…"

She's using my words, I realize. She's using my words, and I'm so fucking proud of her, I could burst. I don't give a shit what her father thinks of me; all I care about is the fact that my wife is protecting *us*: our relationship, our team, our marriage.

"…respectfully," I prompt her.

"…and respectfully," she finishes, "let me know."

Then she marches to the door, opens it, and walks out. And without giving William Salinger another second of my time, I do the same.

"Courtney!" I say, hurrying to catch up with her quick steps on the pebbled driveway. "What the hell just happened?"

"I followed the plan," she says.

"I didn't know you were on board with the plan!"

"Neither was I," she says, and for the first time, I realize she's crying. "But he can't speak to you like that. He can't say those things about you!" She sniffles, and I drop the bags in the middle of the driveway and pull her into my arms. "I was ready for him to say things about *me*, to disrespect *me*. And I could have taken it, Josh. But you?" She shakes her head against my chest. "I couldn't let him keep going." She sniffles again and takes a deep breath before looking up at me with watery eyes. "Team Dalton, right?"

And that's when I know.

That's when I know for sure.

I love her.

I'm in love with Courtney Jane Dalton.

I'm *madly* in love with my wife.

"Right," I say, kissing her on the tip of the nose. "Team Dalton."

She nods before clearing her throat. "It's about a mile back to the station. You up for a walk?"

"After that dramatic exit, it would be a shame to ruin it by going back and asking Gordo for a ride," I say, swiping a tear from her cheek with my thumb.

"He's going to disown me," she says, and I know she's talking about her father.

"Maybe," I say, letting her go and leaning down to pick up the bags.

She sighs as we resume our walk to the end of the driveway. "That stinks, doesn't it?"

"Not as much as enduring that sort of behavior for the next forty years," I say. "But you know what, babe? There'll be an open position for him on Team Dalton when he comes around. And I bet he does, Court. If we stand our ground, I bet he will."

And my wife—who is brave and surprising, nuts and beautiful, and whom I have just realized I love madly—takes one last look at her family home over her shoulder and says, "I hope so."

before walking through the wrought iron gates of her parents' estate and back to the train station with me.

CHAPTER 4
• FINANCES •

"The road is filled with potholes when it comes to managing finances in a new marriage. Three tips that will steer you in the right direction: 1. Don't hide your spending from your partner, 2. Start an emergency fund the day your honeymoon ends, and 3. You'll both make mistakes, so learn early how to forgive."

--Dr. Sydney Morningstar

Courtney

Since our disastrous non-visit with my parents—which resulted in several voice mails that I had to delete because they essentially told me my husband was garbage and my marriage was destined for failure—I have not spoken to my parents.

Part of me hoped that after we'd both had a chance to cool down, they'd call me or I'd call them, and we'd figure out a way to co-exist. Although I agree with Josh that we need to demand the respect we want, I am shaken by what happened in Greenwich. I love my parents, despite the fact that we're not super close. They're still my mom and dad, and without a brother or sister in the mix, all we have is each other.

Except we don't.

Not anymore.

As I was headed out the door this evening, a courier arrived at my office with a certified letter for me. Assuming it was from a client, I signed for it and took it with me, opening the envelope on the elevator. It wasn't from a client. It was from my parents' lawyer and read:

"The trust of Mrs. Courtney Jane Salinger Dalton, heretofore controlled by Mrs. Dalton in concert with her parents, has been remanded into the sole custody of her parents, who will act as caretakers of her estate until such time that Mrs. Dalton may be determined to be of sound mind. Should Mrs. Dalton resume her status as a single woman, thus proving that she has regained control of her senses, such monies as held under the sole protection of her parents shall be returned to her purview and use."

My jaw dropped and my hand started to shake, so I jammed the letter back into the manila envelope and strode out the glass doors of my office building. Gulping back tears, I desperately grasped for enough anger to assuage the ballooning sadness inside of me.

My trust fund, from which I have been able to withdraw freely since I graduated from business school, is now in the sole possession of my parents and closed to me. The money still exists, of course, but only my parents can decide when and if I am ever allowed to touch it again.

I have another option, of course. But it makes me shake with a combination of fury and anguish. They have put a price on my marriage. If I divorce my husband, I can have my trust fund back immediately.

But I will not give him up.

Ever.

Fuck them and their fucking money.

I don't want it. I don't need it.

I am a mess when I open the door to our apartment. Usually, when I get home on a Friday evening, I race down the hallway and into my husband's arms, joyful at the prospect of spending a weekend together.

But tonight?

Tonight, I want to scream. I want to cry. I want to call my parents and tell them that I hate them. I want to rage at them for not even trying to accept my marriage. I want to weep because I can't imagine my life without them, and they are making me choose between them and my husband.

When I step into the living room, Josh looks up, his handsome face breaking into a wide smile. He's wearing jeans and his bare feet are resting on the coffee table. His laptop is perched on his thighs, which tells me he's been busy revising *Miss Gibson Will See You Now* for Simi Frederick's Emerging Playwrights competition. And even though it's been a shit day, I can't help the wave of tenderness, of rightness that crashes over me. Seeing my husband like this? Comfortable in my space, working on his play? It makes my heart fist in a primal way that feels so good it almost hurts.

I won't divorce him.

Not for money.

Not for anything.

"Hey! How was your day?" he asks.

In response, I drop the manila envelope on his lap and stand beside the sofa, arms crossed over my chest, waiting for him to read it.

"What's this?" he asks, pulling out the letter.

"It's from my parents."

He flicks a glance at my face and finally notices that I'm not okay. "Court...what's going on?"

I gulp over the lump in my throat. "Just read it."

Pulling the letter from the envelope, he holds it up and shifts his eyes from my face to the expensive linen paper. As he reads, I watch him—the way his eyebrows furrow and lips part. The way he sucks in a breath of surprise—*Shock? Disgust? Either work for me.*—and lets it go slowly as he finishes reading. Finally, he looks up at me, his face a mixture of anger and concern.

"Are you okay?"

"Sure. Fine," I say, sliding out of my pumps and crossing over to the kitchen. I place my briefcase on the kitchen counter and take a wineglass from the cabinet. "I'm having a drink. Want anything?"

"Um...a Heineken?"

I never had beer in my fridge before living with Josh, but when I open the door and see his beer bottles lined up next to my bottle of Sauvignon Blanc, tears spring to my eyes because it looks so right, so perfect.

Suggesting that I divorce him is profane.
Blackmailing me into it is reprehensible.

I will never forgive them.

I blink back the tears and pour myself a large glass of wine, chugging most of it before refilling the glass with what's left in the bottle. Before I can raise it to my lips again, Josh is standing across the kitchen counter from me.

"Bullshit."

I pause with the bathtub-sized goblet halfway to my lips. "What?"

"Bullshit, you're fine." He reaches for my glass, gently pulls it from my fingers, and places it on the counter. "You're about to drink half a bottle of wine in sixty seconds."

I lock eyes with him, about to tell him to leave me alone to do what I want, but my whole body—every single muscle inside of me—tenses to the point of pain and I can't talk. I can't do anything but stand here frozen.

"Court," he says softly, stepping around the counter, "that letter…was awful. Talk to me."

And just like that, I uncoil.

I unravel.

I fall apart.

I dissolve into uncontrollable sobs, which makes it hard to breathe and impossible to speak. My parents, who weren't perfect, but were always *there*, are *not there* anymore. They have deserted me.

The keening sound I finally make feels surreal and far away, and my now-jelly-like muscles feel weak and limp. But before I fall, Josh's arms—strong, sure arms—are suddenly around me, are lifting me up, are carrying me away.

I burrow my face into Josh's warm neck and try to catch my breath, but I can't.

"Baby…Courtney…breathe."

His voice, low and soothing, tells me to draw air, and I try to comply, but my first gasps are short and shallow.

"You're hyperventilating, Court. Take a deep breath. Come on, baby. A deep one."

I turn my head and look up, into his bright blue eyes, focusing on them as I force my lungs to relax and fill them with air.

"That's it. Again, Court. Come on. Again."

Cradled in his arms on the side of our bed, I take another deep breath, holding the air inside of my burning lungs before slowly letting it go. When I do, a sob, more normal and less harsh, multiplies into many, and here I am: nestled in my husband's arms, wearing pantyhose and a business suit, crying like a baby.

I don't know when, but eventually, he transitions me to my side and lies down beside me, pulling my body against his and holding on tight. He doesn't say anything, just keeps repeating "it's okay" and "it'll be alright," except I don't know if it will be okay or alright. My parents have abjured me, and the pain of their rejection is almost unbearable.

But I will not give him up.

If I must, I will make my life with him, and without them.

I just wish it didn't have to be this way.

When my sobs slow down into hiccups and sniffles, Josh finally speaks.

"I've never seen you like this," he says, taking a deep

breath. It pushes his front into my back and I close my eyes, grateful for the intimacy of it. It's like his heart is nudging mine.

"I've...n-never...b-been...disowned," I somehow manage to choke out.

"I can't believe this is forever," he says, his breath warm on the back of my neck. "They're just angry. They're being hateful because you wouldn't stand there and take their abuse. Because you've broken away from them and don't want to live under their control anymore. But you're their only daughter. They'll soften over time. I'm sure of it."

I close my eyes, burrowing into him. The money? I can live without it. But the fact that my parents would try to make me choose between them and my husband? It's devastating to me and I can't imagine a time—whether they "soften" or not—that I won't be hurt by their words and actions. I can't see a future with them in it and it hurts me.

"Did your grandfather disown your Aunt Lucy?" Josh asks.

"N-No," I sniffle. "But in f-fairness, Josh, she m-married a l-lord."

"True," he says softly.

I realize how my words might sound to him—like he's not as good as British nobility—and rush to reassure him. "I don't care that you're not a lord. I want you just the way you are. I'm not—I mean, I don't want a divorce. I d-don't want to l-lose you."

"You won't," he says, and I hear the oh-so-slight whisper of relief in his voice, which comforts me. "I don't want a divorce either."

"I just c-can't believe they would d-do this. It's so f-final. It's so…ugly."

He waits a beat, then says, "Can I ask you something?"

"Sure."

He takes a deep breath. "What are you more upset about? That you don't have access to your trust anymore, or——?"

"How can you even ask me that?"

"I'm just making sure."

"Fuck the money!" I cry. "I don't want it. They can have it!" More tears stream down my cheeks. "I c-can't believe they'd try to b-blackmail me into d-divorcing you."

He hugs me close. "Shh, baby. It's okay."

"It's not okay! It's manipulative. It's despicable." I fight to breathe deeply, and it isn't pretty, but I finally fill my diaphragm with a jagged, choppy breath. "Do they honestly th-think I'd d-divorce you for m-money?"

"They had to believe it was possible."

"Well, it's not," I answer.

"Maybe this is a test? To see how serious you are about our marriage?"

"If that's true, it's unforgivable."

We're both silent for a few minutes until Josh asks, "How much are we talking about, exactly?"

"In my trust?"

"Yeah."

"I don't know. Six million dollars. Give or take."

I hear and feel him suck in so sharply, the *whoosh* on my neck makes me freeze. I have shocked him.

"Whoa," he gasps. "Six...*million*? Six million dollars?"

That's not even all of it. It doesn't include whatever my parents planned to give me, plus assets like the house in Connecticut, the apartment in New York, the ski lodge in—

"You're willing to give that up?" he asks, his voice a low whisper of awe. "For *me*?"

My eyes burn with tears again and I blink them, holding them closed and savoring the deep timbre of his beloved voice.

Beloved. Loved.

And that's when I realize it:

I'm in love with my husband.

I love him.

I love Josh Dalton.

Completely. Beyond reason. And certainly beyond any dollar amount.

There's strength in the knowledge of what truly matters to me. Josh matters. He matters the most.

"Mm-hm," I murmur, turning in his arms to face him. "I'm willing to give it up."

His eyes search mine intently. "Why?"

Am I ready to tell him I love him? I've only just realized it myself.

"You're my husband," I say, chickening out on the words perched on the tip of my tongue. "We're married."

"Only just," he whispers, his eyebrows knitting together with doubt.

I lean forward and press my lips to his, moving them softly, loving his tenderly. Though he holds me tightly, he doesn't try to deepen the kiss. He wants an answer.

"It's not a matter of *how long* we've been married," I say. "It doesn't matter if we've been married for an hour or a century. We're together. We're promised forever. Team Dalton, remember?"

He bites his bottom lip before letting it go. "Yeah…but it feels like you're giving up so much more than I am."

"I'm not," I insist. "It's just money."

"*Just money*," he scoffs. "You wouldn't say that if you'd ever gone without."

Honestly, I don't want to talk about it anymore. Since I kissed him, I can feel his hardness prodding against my belly, and I want him just as much as he wants me. I need to feel close to him right now. I need something physical right now—something real, something I can touch and hold and feel. Something to act as immediate ballast against my parents' terrific viciousness.

"Having you is everything," I say. "I wanted marriage, remember? I was willing to make sacrifices to have it."

I purposely breathe in deeply so that my nipples, which are puckering inside of my thin bra and silk blouse, rub against his T-shirt.

"Mrs. Dalton," he says, flicking a glance at the place where our chests are touching. "By any chance, are you getting turned on?"

"Could be," I say, arching my back. "I don't want to talk about my parents anymore."

"Okay…" He licks his lips as his fingers move to the buttons on my blouse. "Then you have way too many clothes on."

"True. Give a girl a hand?"

He's naughty as he undoes my buttons, boldly slipping his palm into my bra and caressing my nipple into an even tighter point.

"Take off my pants," he orders.

My hands move to do his bidding, quickly unfastening the metal rivet at his waist and pulling down the copper zipper. His cock is rigid under his boxers, throbbing with life and want of me, which makes me moan with longing.

"I need you," I say, grasping at the elastic of his underwear and pulling at it.

He chuckles, the sound deep and cocky. His hand slides away from my breast and he stands up beside the bed, looking down at me as he shucks off his jeans and underwear, then reaches behind his neck and pulls off his T-shirt. He throws it to the floor, gloriously naked, grinning at me.

"Now you," he tells me.

I pull my half-unbuttoned blouse and jacket over my head awkwardly, unfasten my bra, then kneel on the bed and reach behind my waist to unzip my skirt. When I lie back, my husband pulls it off, trailing his hands up my nylon-covered legs.

"What's the point of these?"

He rests the foot of his palm flush against my pussy and I can barely focus on his question because he presses down, and it makes my clit quiver.

"W-What?"

"Pantyhose. What's the point?"

"I don't know the fucking point," I grumble. "Just get them off!"

He laughs at me, and I lean up on my elbows to reprimand him, only to find that his cock is so hard and high, it's practically parallel against his belly. My eyes widen and my mouth waters, but I'm quickly distracted. Slipping his thumbs into my panties, he yanks, pulling the last of my clothing to my knees and then off altogether.

Kneeling on the floor between my thighs, he buries his head between my legs, his hands pushing them apart. With unbelievable accuracy, his wet, hot tongue lands flush on my throbbing clit and I fall back onto the bed, closing my eyes and sighing.

Josh doesn't know this, but he is the first man with whom I've been comfortable enough to have oral sex, which means I have nothing to compare him to. But I am fairly certain he's a genius at what he's doing, because I have never felt anything remotely as awesome as his tongue lapping at my clit. I grab at his head, threading my fingers through his dark hair.

When I am about to fall apart, his tongue disappears, but before I can fully open my eyes, his hot, hard cock slides inside of me to the hilt.

"Fuuuuuck," I moan, forcing my eyes open to look up at him. "Josh."

"Yeah, baby…I'm here," he pants, leaning down to kiss me.

I can taste myself on his lips and tongue, tangy and

sweet, and it's so hot, I swear my orgasm starts there. It builds from the pumping friction of his cock thrusting in and out of my aroused body, from the sweetness of his kisses, from the slick heat of his skin against mine, and—most of all—from the feelings I have for him. From the knowledge that we chose each other. It is a litany in my head. A prayer so sacred, I cannot even share it yet with him:

I love you. I love you. I love you.

IloveyouIloveyouIloveyouIloveyou...

Again and again, my body rises to meet his. My pussy clenches his cock, gloving it like a second skin. My muscles contract in concert with his. And when we climax, we come together, grasping and crying out in ecstasy.

And when we are sated, we lie down side-by-side and hold on tight.

We belong to each other. In making love, we have reaffirmed our bond, our promise, our faith in the future we will build and share together, with or without my parents and their money.

Cradled in his arms, sleep comes quickly after the pain of betrayal and the sweetness of loving, my last thought before I close my eyes bringing me full circle:

I will not give him up.

Ever.

***

Josh

"Court?" I call into the bedroom. "My mom wants to say hi."

"Coming!" she answers, leaving the bathroom with one towel wrapped around her body and another wrapped around her head like a turban. She grins at me, and Jesus, I am a sap for this woman. I can feel that smile everywhere and I'm grinning back at her like a fool.

I cover the mouthpiece of my phone. "Do you want to get dressed first, Mrs. Dalton?"

"Nope. I'm good." She reaches for the phone, sitting on the bed and settling back against the pillows. "Joanie? Hi! How are you?"

She shoos me out of the room with a little wave, and I step back into the back hallway, quietly delighted by the sound of my bride giggling on the phone with my mom. After what happened on Friday night—when she lost it so completely after receiving her parents' letter—I wasn't sure what the weekend would hold. But she wrote back to their lawyer yesterday, declaring that there would be no divorce and that she was in full retention of her faculties. She also wrote that she would not contest her parents' decision, which, I have to believe, is going to make them ballistic. I'm fairly certain they wanted Courtney to make a scene, or divorce me, or act out in such a way that gave them cause to think she was crazy. I'm so proud of her for behaving with grace and sense under pressure. Honest to God, I'm not sure I could have done the same.

That said, and thank God, it hasn't been an issue for me; my parents have been awesome about everything—way more accepting and accommodating than I expected. I anticipated disappointment and tears, but when we called them two weeks ago, both of my parents were joyful about our news—eager to speak with Courtney and get to know her better. They sent flowers and an expensive-for-them bottle of champagne a few days later, and we skyped with them to have a virtual toast. Last Sunday, Courtney chatted with my mom for over an hour, and I loved it that she was so willing to hop on the phone again today. Lord only knows what they're talking about, but it means a lot to me that they're bonding.

Courtney must have her laptop out in the bedroom, because when I sit down at the kitchen counter and open mine, there's a text from her: *Your mom is the cutest!* I send back a smiley face, and she writes again: *I just told her we're coming for Thanksgiving and she's freaking out. It's going to be great!* With this text is a Delta link that she also shares, and I click on it, remembering that she was going to make a reservation for us.

The flights are great; we're leaving the Wednesday before Thanksgiving at 11:00am and arriving in Minneapolis at 1:30pm, and we fly out on Sunday at 1:00pm and get back to New York by 5:00pm. Amazing. When I have to travel anywhere, I'm usually flying out at six o'clock in the morning or arriving after midnight because it's so much cheaper.

Hmm. That makes me wonder…

My eyes skim down to the total cost for the trip, and I immediately understand why the flights are so fantastic. Courtney's booked us in first class and the two round-trip tickets cost almost three thousand dollars.

"Fuck me, " I mutter, sweating a little as I rub my jaw.

The last time I flew home, I fare-hunted for weeks until I found a round-trip seat for under four hundred dollars. I left at 5:55am and flew back on a really awful red-eye. There's a reason these flights are almost eight times as expensive.

Sliding off the kitchen stool, I peek into the bedroom, making eye contact with my wife. She grins at me and covers the phone receiver. "Everything okay?"

"Yeah. Um…when did you buy those plane tickets?"

"Today. This morning."

"Huh. Okay."

Today. Exactly the word I was hoping she *wouldn't* say.

Today. Two days *after* she lost her trust fund.

All we have right now is her salary and mine. And that's to float our super expensive apartment, her car, garage parking, and all of the other expenses that Courtney used to supplement with her trust. Maybe we can still afford first class air tickets on some tony flight, but maybe we can't. Maybe we shouldn't. Maybe we need to change the way we spend and save a little here and there. I'd feel a whole lot better if we talked about it.

"Your mom's telling me how she makes the turkey!" she squeals.

"Fun!" I say, trying not to show the panic I feel. "Come find me when you're done, okay?"

She nods and smiles. "I will."

I back out of our room, thinking about the fact that my wife has never had to curb her spending. She's never had to choose cheaper, less convenient flights because they'd save her a little money. She's never had to think about how much she's spending against how much she has.

I sit back down at the kitchen counter, about to research other, cheaper fares when my phone buzzes with a message. Thinking it's Courtney, I flip over the phone right away, but my heart sinks.

It's not from my wife, but my ex.

Sam.

I haven't heard from Sam for about a month, since Courtney and I returned from our honeymoon and settled down in her apartment. By design, I've only shown up at the New Dramatists workshops a couple of times and only when I knew Sam was teaching. Why? For two reasons: one, because I really don't want to talk about her feelings for me, and two, because it feels really wrong to spend any time with Sam when I'm married to Courtney.

Call me a chickenshit. I can take it. It's the truth. I don't want to deal with Sam, so I've gone out of my way to avoid her, and—thank God!—it's been working...until now.

Clicking on the text, I open it up and brace myself for drama, but I'm pleasantly surprised.

Hey, Josh...did I hear my good friend – and his new wife – are having a housewarming party?

She's right. We are.

Courtney and I have been married a month, we've told our parents and our closest friends, and last week, Courtney suggested we have a little cocktail party at our apartment so we could meet each other's friends and announce our marriage.

She sent an invite to Dina, of course, plus some friends from college and a few work colleagues. I sent invites to my old roommates—Max, Mike, and Jenna—but not to Sam.

For one thing, she declared her undying love for me, and I ignored it. Plus, even though we used to be good friends, after dating, I really wasn't sure where we stood anymore. Not to mention, Max is coming, and I didn't want him to have to see Sam if he was still upset about their break-up.

But now? Seeing this pretty innocuous message from Sam? I wonder if I acted hastily. Or punitively. Maybe I should have included her. Hell, maybe she went on a couple of drunken rampages while she was texting me and has been feeling as awkward as me ever since.

Hey, stranger! I reply. *Yep. A small cocktail party…the Friday after next.*

Not working on Fridays anymore? she texts back.

I type: *Nope. I'm off on weekends now.*

I'm gonna kill the elephant in the room, okay? I'm sorry things got so weird between us. I've been trying to give you space.

I flick a glance to the bedroom, but I can still hear Courtney talking to my mom, so I write back: *Yeah. Those texts were pretty intense.*

I'm really sorry, Josh. I mean it. I was going through a thing. Water under the bridge?

My instinct actually tells me that we can't call it a "thing" and shove it under the carpet without a conversation to clear the air, but remember that streak of chickenshit I mentioned before? Yeah. That wins for now.

Sure. I type back, breathing a sigh of relief. *Not to throw salt in the wound...but, how's Max doing?*

No salt. He's good. He's already dating someone else.

Really? I'm surprised. Max seemed so gaga over Sam.

Yeah. Remember Mia? The girl who took the couch? Well...she was there for Max after the break-up and they're a thing now.

Huh. Okay. That was quick...but love often blooms under duress.

Are you still living there? I ask her.

LOL. Yeah. Now, I'm on the couch. She's in the bedroom with Max.

Whoa. That must be weird.

But in the world I *used* to live in, you tolerate all sorts of weird if it means you've got a roof over your head and you're free to pursue your passion. No joke, I once slept on the couch in a living room used as practice space for a band. I wasn't even allowed to pull out the sofa bed until 1:30am every morning, because that's when rehearsals ended. And you know what? I was grateful for that bed every night.

Still, it's got to be awkward, I think.

Are you okay with that?

It's fine, she writes back. *You and I lived together after we broke up, remember?*

Yes, I do. And all the while I thought we were both happy being friends.

Not awkward?

Nope. You know how it is.

I do and I don't. I wasn't in love with Sam, so seeing her with Max didn't hurt, it made sense. From everything

I've gathered, Sam wasn't in love with Max either, so maybe seeing him with Mia is actually...comforting. Like, she didn't break his heart in two. He was able to move on. Any guilt she feels for breaking up with him is taken away.

And if Sam and Max can bury the hatchet so simply, she and I should too.

You should come to Courtney's and my housewarming thing. Friday after next. Check in with Max and those guys. They have the details.

Sure! she types back. *Sounds fun! Can I bring anything?*

"Josh? Your mom wants to say good bye!"

I whip my neck around to see Courtney standing in the living room with towels still wrapped around her body and her head. I fumble with my phone, feeling nervous, feeling caught. It slips from my fingers and I juggle it like a clown before I manage to shove it in my back pocket.

"Bravo!" Courtney giggles. "Did I startle you?"

"No," I say, circling the kitchen counter and holding out my hand for the phone. But I know my cheeks are flushed. I can feel the heat in them, and it tells me that I don't feel right talking to Sam after all that stuff she said about us.

"Hey, Mom," I say, as Courtney gives my face a once-over. She raises one eyebrow for a second, then flashes me her boobs with a lusty chuckle, before turning around and heading back to the bedroom. "How's it going?"

"Joshua. Isn't she something? We just love her already!"

"Yeah. She's the best."

Did Courtney sense something was off? I really didn't

want to tell her about Sam's texts, but now I'm wondering if I should have. Nah. She flashed me. She was being playful. We're good.

"And you're coming for Thanksgiving! Oh, fer fun, honey! Daddy and I can't wait to meet her!"

"I know. It's going to be great, Mom."

"And we'll all attend services on Wednesday evening and Sunday morning?"

I briefly think about our conversation on the train two weeks ago. "She isn't a regular church-goer, but I don't think she'll mind."

"Not a church-goer?" My mother's voice is genuinely perplexed. Suddenly, she lowers it and asks, "Is she Jewish? There are many Jewish people in New York and it's a proud tradition of faith that—"

"No, Mom. She's not Jewish. She just doesn't go to church very much."

"Why not?"

"I don't know. She goes on Christmas Eve and Easter."

"Oh. So, she's a lapsed Catholic?"

"Nope." She didn't know what transubstantiation was. No way she attended CCD. "I don't think so."

"Well, that's a riddle we'll just have to solve when you two are visiting."

Again, my mother surprises me. This could have been a real deal-breaker for uber-Christian Joanie Dalton, but I'm pleasantly surprised by how accepting she is.

"You're awesome, Mom."

"You seem happy, Joshua. That makes me happy."

We say our goodbyes and I promise to call again next Sunday, then I put the cordless phone back in its cradle and look for Courtney in the bedroom. I find her dressed in shorts and a T-shirt, sitting at her dressing table and brushing out her long blonde hair.

"Hey, babe," I say, "thanks for being so nice to my mom."

"I like her," Courtney says, spinning around to grin at me. "She has some good stories about you."

"Like what?" I sit on the bed, smiling back at her.

"She told me about the little black and white kitty you brought home from the woods. But it wasn't a kitty, it was a baby—"

"Skunk," I finish for her. "The hissing, growling, and stench gave it away."

She chuckles, then goes back to brushing her hair. "Thanksgiving should be fun."

"Er. Yeah. Definitely." I pause for a second, then say: "Um, actually, I wanted to talk to you about that."

"Okay." She turns around again, her smile fading. "Is everything okay?"

I don't know how to say this. I want to strike the right tone: conversational, not censorious, especially since we mostly live on her salary.

"The tickets. They were…expensive."

She shrugs. "Not really."

"Babe, the last time I flew to Minnesota, I spent four hundred dollars. The tickets you bought are almost three *thousand* dollars."

"Wow! You got a deal, huh?"

"Yeah," I say. "I sat in economy and left at six o'clock in the morning, but yeah. The tickets were about eleven hundred dollars less."

"Josh," she says, turning back around to face herself in the mirror. "You don't need to worry. I can afford it. *We* can afford it."

"Can we?" I ask gently. "*Without* your trust?"

Her lips flatten into a tight line and her eyes get wary.

"Courtney, I just…I don't know if you've ever had to live frugally, but without your trust, maybe we should try to live within our means, you know? Maybe even save a little for a rainy day?"

"Believe me," she says, "three thousand dollars *is* within our means."

"But does it need to be? When we could get there just as easily for eight hundred dollars?"

"Not *just as easily*," she says, sweeping her still-damp hair into a ponytail and fastening it with a velvet elastic. "At the crack of dawn. We'll be exhausted. And coach? No offense, but it sucks. It's so crowded. And stressful."

Compromises, Josh. Marriage is about compromises.

"Okay," I say, switching gears as I think of another way to cut costs. "Then, you know how we were going to go out to the Hamptons next weekend?"

"To see Dina and the girls? Yep. I can't wait!"

"And you said the helicopter ride each way would be $525 each?"

She nods. "Yeah."

"Well, I propose we take the car that you already own, for which you already pay parking, and drive out there instead."

"*Drive* to the Hamptons?" she asks, looking at me like I'm crazy. "On a *Friday*?"

"Yep. It'll save us $2100."

"Exactly what you'd save exchanging the Delta tickets for coach," she observes.

"And I don't mind driving. You can read or watch a movie...or take a nap."

She sighs, looking annoyed, but not angry. "You feel strongly about this?"

"I feel strongly that until we understand where your trust filled in the gaps in your lifestyle, that we rein things in a little."

She stares at me for a second. "For the record, Josh? I don't like this. It feels a little bit like you're trying to control me."

"I'm not," I assure her. "I just want us to be smart about our choices."

"*Drive* to the Hamptons," she says again, this time with a sour puss on her sweet lips.

"With the hottest chauffeur ever," I say, trying to lighten the mood.

That makes her grin. "Fine. But I don't want you policing every dollar we spend. I can't live like that. That's just...icky."

"I'll make you a deal," I say. "If it costs over a thousand dollars, we talk first. Can you live with that?"

She tilts her head to the side for a second, then nods. "I guess I can live with that."

"I'm crazy about you," I say, reaching to pull her off the dressing table chair, and onto the bed with me.

"I bet you say that to all the girls," she says, letting me roll her onto her back and tug her T-shirt over her head.

"Only the ones I'm married to," I say, leaning down to kiss her, all thoughts of airfares, Thanksgiving, of Sam, and the Hamptons, fading away as I pull my wife into my arms.

CHAPTER 5
• SOCIAL LIFE •

"Your new marriage may be the epicenter of your universe, but for your friends, some of whom may still be single, adjusting to your married status can take time on their part, and patience on yours."
--Dr. Sydney Morningstar

<u>Josh</u>

When I told Courtney I was happy to drive us out to the Hamptons, I had no idea what kind of car she owned; I only knew that by driving us, I would be saving us over two thousand dollars, and at the time, that was all that mattered.

Until the guy at the garage brought her car around.

It turns out my girl owns a black Audi A8, and besides her face, I swear to God, it's the prettiest thing I've ever seen.

I'm not even *into* cars, really.

But this car is my *dream* car.

Ever since I saw Jason Statham driving one on two wheels like a total motherfucking badass in *Transporter 3*, I've been a bona fide Audi devotee. In fact, if one of my plays ever started making money, a used Audi would have been the first luxury purchase on my list.

And now I'm about to drive one.

"Baby," I say reverently, trailing a finger over the shiny black hood of her car, "you have an Audi."

"Huh?"

She looks up from her phone where she's been texting Dina for the past ten minutes. Between Courtney's monthlong assignment in England and Dina renting a house in the Hamptons for the month of July and staying out there every weekend, they've barely seen each other this summer. I know they're excited to get together again. Frankly, I'm looking forward to seeing Dina too. She's pretty awesome, and without her gentle interference last spring, my wife and I may not have found our way to each other.

"This car rocks."

"Oh, thanks. My dad said it had a good safety rating."

Safety rating? This car is sex on wheels! Who cares about the safety rating?

I put our bags in the trunk, while she slides into the passenger seat and closes her door. When I sit down beside her, I'm practically humming with pleasure. The tan leather seats are soft and supple, and the interior looks (and smells) new. Brand new. Like it's never been driven.

"How often do you drive this?"

"Hmm? Oh. Well, I prefer to take the train out to Greenwich, and when *I can*—" She gives me a meaningful look. "—I like to get where I'm going faster than a car can get me there. So…not much."

Since our chat last weekend about being a little more frugal with our spending and agreeing to touch base with each other about purchases over $1000, my bride has been slightly salty with me when it comes to money or travel. I know she doesn't like it that I commented on how she spends her money, but I swear I'm not trying to control her. I'm concerned about unexpected expenses that I won't be able to handle on my own, and worried that she has this mindset that there are inexhaustible funds at her disposal whenever she wants something.

Our combined salaries are good. Even great. She makes a little over two hundred grand a year, and with my changed hours, I make about sixty. But we also live in Manhattan, in a really luxurious building. We eat out whenever we like, and Courtney has expensive taste in clothes, shoes, and bags. We can afford our apartment, car, and most of our day-to-day lifestyle, I'm pretty sure. But first-class air tickets and round-trip helicopter rides to the Hamptons are luxuries that we might want to put on the back burner until Courtney adjusts to not having her trust as a financial security blanket.

Not to mention, she has this insanely gorgeous car! Why would we take a stupid helicopter anywhere when we could take her Audi?

I glance over at her, but she's engrossed in texting, so I don't force her to share my enjoyment as I turn over the engine and rev the motor a little. Oh, man. This drive? *It's going to be epic*, I think as I pull out of the garage.

Four hours later, I can confirm that it's been epic. Epically *slow*. According to Courtney's cutting-edge GPS, Dina's house in East Hampton is only 115 miles from our apartment building in Manhattan, but we left at five-fifteen, it's a little after nine o'clock now, and we're *still* ten miles away, sitting in stop-and-go traffic on the Montauk Parkway.

Courtney sighs loudly for the fourth or fifth time in ten minutes and I turn to her.

"What?"

"I didn't say anything."

"Your sighs speak louder than words."

"And what are they saying, pray tell? Are they saying the word '*helicopter*,' by any chance?"

Okay. So, maybe I didn't realize that Friday evening traffic from New York City to the Hamptons was as bad as it is. But, fuck, before now I didn't have the money for luxuries like "summer-shares." I was lucky to have a mattress under my body and a pillow beneath my head. How was I supposed to know that the Long Island Expressway would be a veritable parking lot on a Friday afternoon?

"No," I answer. "They're saying that Friday night traffic to the Hamptons is a bitch."

She scoffs. "*Everyone* knows that."

"Not me," I say, clocking her attitude for the umpteenth time since we got in the car, and frankly, I'm not impressed. For four hours, she's texted her friends, fiddled with the radio, read *Cosmopolitan,* and surfed the internet. *I've* been the one dealing with the lunatic drivers surrounding us, but *she's* the one copping an attitude.

Not that I know a ton about summer shares, but I guess it's quite popular for ten girls to rent a five-bedroom house in the Hamptons from Memorial Day to Labor Day, each girl paying one-tenth of the total cost, and having a bed and half a closet that's all hers for the duration of the rental.

As long as it's okay with your roommate, you can share your bed with your boyfriend or another guest, or you can—with your housemates' approval—sublet your bed to a mutual friend of the group for one-off weekends that you can't be there (which is what Dina's roommate is doing for us). But the girls generally leave work after lunch on Fridays, arrive at the house well before dinner, have cocktails and dinner with whomever is there, and head out clubbing around nine with whatever entourage they've assembled for the weekend.

Courtney looks at her phone and sighs again. "We missed cocktails and dinner."

"Sorry," I say stiffly, thinking that she's acting like a brat.

This isn't a side of Courtney I've seen much of before now. When she and Dina would come into Tidewaters, she was always polite and gracious. Even when we were out in Connecticut at the posh country club wedding of her parents' friends' daughter, she didn't act like this. I'm not a fan of this self-centered princess attitude she's got going on. Not at all.

"Dina just texted. She, Morgan, and Reagan challenged the guys to a game of speed quarters, but I think they're just killing time waiting for us. The rest already left for the Beacon."

"What's the Beacon?"

"It's a cool place in Sag Harbor," she mutters.

"Wait," I say, "are we driving somewhere else once we get there?"

"Maybe. Yeah."

"But I've been driving for almost four hours."

"That's not my fault," she mutters.

I eek off the highway behind a bunch of other cars who are also, apparently, headed to East Hampton. "Well, *I'm* not going anywhere."

"What do you mean?"

"I mean...we're almost there. We drove four hours to get there. Why would we get right back in the car to go somewhere else? It doesn't make any sense."

She crosses her arms over her chest and looks out the window, ignoring me.

"Court?"

"Because that's what we do!" She huffs loudly. "God! It's bad enough that we're late, but now they're sitting there, waiting for us, Josh. Wouldn't it be an asshole move to get there and then *not* go out?"

"I guess you'd know," I say.

"What does *that* mean?"

"It means that this is all new to me, babe," I say, an edge in my voice that I'm unable to control. "And you're not exactly making it fun for anyone."

The light at the end of the exit ramp turns green and I move forward, finally nearing the little town of East Hampton. We're moving along a little faster now, traffic thinning out as cars reach their destinations. I stop at a red light in the village and note the hustle and bustle of Friday night revelry. Restaurants with white twinkle lights serve patrons seated at café tables on the sidewalks, and groups of girls in short, trendy sundresses walk in groups, laughing and talking. A couple crosses in front of us, the guy wearing pink shorts and a white, buttoned-down shirt with rolled-up sleeves and an embroidered belt. I think about the T-shirts and gym shorts in my duffel bag and know I've under-packed.

"Sorry that sitting in a car for four hours and missing dinner has made me grumpy," Courtney whines, "but we could have been here by six if we'd just kept our Blade reservations."

"You know what?" I say, snapping at her just as the light turns green. "Let's talk about that. Let's talk about the fact that you blithely drop two thousand dollars on round-trip helicopter tickets to visit your friends, who are staying a few hours away, *in the same state*. That's nuts, Courtney. You are *totally* out of touch with reality if you think that's necessary."

"*I'm* out of touch with reality?" she says. "*You're* the one that insisted we *drive*...to the *Hamptons*...on a *Friday*...in *July*. If anyone's nuts in this car, *baby*, it's you!"

"You're a spoiled brat," I mutter.

"And you're a midwestern hick!" she snipes back.

We drive in silence for several minutes, neither of us saying anything, but my chest feels tight and my jaw hurts when I finally unclench it a couple of miles up the road. Is that what she really thinks of me? That I'm a "midwestern hick"? It hurts more than I would have guessed to hear her say it. Fuck. It hurts a lot.

We're driving in utter darkness now; the road we're looking for is about a mile and a half up on the right.

Courtney sniffles softly beside me, and I look over to see her swipe at her eyes, but I don't reach for her hand or offer any comforting words. Her feelings are hurt? Good. Mine are too. And *I'm* the one about to enter foreign territory. It would have been nice to feel secure with my wife and confident about our marriage while meeting her friends for the first time. Instead, we're in a fight and I feel like— like a country bumpkin.

In fairness? I guess that's what I am. For all that I came to New York when I was eighteen, and have lived there for eight years, I'm *from* Minnetonka, Minnesota. And sure, we were comfortable there. My family lived in a perfectly nice house and each of my parents drove a decent American car, but we didn't belong to one of the country clubs in Minneapolis or up in Wayzata. When we "vacationed," it was mostly to my grandparents' lake house up in Duluth, and when we celebrated special occasions, we had a BBQ in the backyard, or reserved a table at the Redstone Steakhouse downtown.

I didn't grow up in the sort of upper-upper class family that Courtney did; nowhere near it. But before today, it didn't really matter all that much to me. I guess because I didn't think it mattered much to her.

And now I wonder if it does.

Is she embarrassed to introduce me to her friends as her husband? As her "midwestern hick" of a husband? My heart squeezes and I gulp over the swelling lump in my throat. It hurts like hell to think that she's ashamed of me. It hurts and it pisses me off.

"Feel free to go out with your friends tonight," I say. "I won't be joining you."

"I'll…stay with you," she says, her voice thin and tinged with misery, which gives me a tiny bit of satisfaction.

"No," I say firmly. "You should go out."

As we turn into the driveway, she puts her hand on my arm.

"I didn't mean it, Josh," she whispers. "I don't know why I said that. I don't think of you like that."

"It's fine," I say, pulling her car behind a Jaguar and cutting the engine. "I didn't mean it either."

She stares at me in the darkness, her face lit by the ambient light from the dashboard and a floodlight on the garage which we've tripped whilst pulling in. She doesn't smile. In fact, her lovely face looks…sad. Possibly even as sad as mine.

The front door opens, and I hear someone—who sounds very much like Dina—yell, "Courtney's here! You guys, she's *finally* here!"

"It'll be okay," she says, pulling her hand away and sliding out the passenger door to greet her friends.

My heart's as heavy as stone as I watch her go.

On some level and to some degree, we both meant what we said.

And it doesn't feel okay at all.

***

Courtney

Smile, Courtney, smile.

I force myself to wave at Dina, Morgan, and Reagan, who are squeezed together in the front doorway of their summer house, waving and squealing at me.

"She's here, you guys!" "Finally!" "Court's here! Court's here!"

These are the same girls with whom I've shared a house in the Hamptons for the past four years of my life. We've BBQ'd, caroused, and suntanned together. I've held back their hair while they puked and acted as late-night wingman more than once. And now I'm here with Josh, my husband—the first to be married in our tribe.

"Hey, ladies!" I greet them, adopting a cheerfulness I don't feel.

"OMG, Courtney! Where's your man?" asks Morgan, a childhood acquaintance from Greenwich and classmate at prep school. She's a lawyer at one of Manhattan's most prestigious firms.

"He's in the car," I say. "Long drive. He'll be out in a minute."

"We're literally *dying* to meet him," says Reagan, a sexy redhead, who's a buyer for Saks.

I meet Dina's eyes, and since she's my best friend and knows me way better than these other girls, her eyes narrow a touch. "Everything okay?"

"Yeah," I say, reaching to hug her so she can't scan my face again. "For sure. Just…a lot of traffic."

"Who decided that *driving* was a good idea in the first place?" she whispers in my ear.

"Who do you think?" I whisper back.

"Mmm," she hums, and I know she's putting everything together in her head. She lets me go and glances over my shoulder at the car where Josh is—presumably, since I haven't heard his door open and close—still brooding. "You go inside with these two. I'll go say hi."

As Dina makes her way across the driveway to check in with Josh, Morgan and Reagan pull me into the house.

"You've got to get dressed!"

"We'll help you."

"Everyone already went to the Beacon."

"Except us. We waited for you!"

With our arms linked together, we walk into the great room of the house, which is decorated in bright white and seaside teal tones, perfect for a summer house.

"Courts, remember Bennett?" asks Morgan, a slight tease in her voice.

My breath catches and my cheeks color as Bennett Foster, my quasi-boyfriend from high school, stands up from the couch with a beer in his hand.

"Hey, CJ," he says, using my father's nickname for me, which he always thought was amusing…likely because I hated it so much. He wasn't an especially nice boyfriend, but it still stung when he cheated on me with a mutual friend.

"Bennett."

"Long time, no see. Gimme a hug."

He reaches over a glass coffee table covered in empty beer bottles and I lean forward so that only our cheeks touch as we briefly embrace each other.

"Lookin' good, CJ," he murmurs near my ear, so softly

no one can hear.

I jerk away from him, feeling uncomfortable.

"Off the market now, huh?" He grins. "Heard you got married."

"Ya sure, ya betcha," says a voice from behind me. "Fer sure she did. All married up now."

Bennett's eyes widen, sliding from mine to someone standing behind me, just as a strong arm encircles my waist and the flattened palm of a masculine hand lands meaningfully on my belly.

"You're the lucky guy, I presume?" Bennett's gaze rests on my stomach for a moment before he looks up at my husband again.

"Ya got dat right," he says, holding out the hand that isn't clasping me. "Josh Dalton."

And it's right about now I realize he's speaking with the most exaggerated midwestern accent he can probably muster. It's about ten times stronger than his mother's and that's saying something.

"Bennett Foster."

"Great t'meetcha," says Josh. "Okay, den. Well, dis here house is sumptin', eh?"

Bennett's staring at Josh like he is both fascinated and horrified. "Where did you two… meet?"

"At da bar," says Josh.

"Dabar?" clarifies Morgan, blinking her eyes. "Is that a new place?"

"Da…bar," enunciates Josh, adding a fake chuckle. "Where ya' get da drinks? Oh-fer-geez, I think they wanna hear how we met, hunny. Ya wanna tell 'em or me?"

At this point, I can barely understand what the hell he's saying.

I reach for his hand and try to pull it from my stomach, but he tightens it, so I pat it twice like we're all having fun. "You guys, Josh went to NYU. He's a playwright…and right now, he's playing all of you."

"Just kidding around a little," says Josh, in a low, sexy voice, now devoid of all Minnesota affections. He lets go of me and steps forward, holding his hand out to Morgan and Reagan. "Let's try this again. Josh Dalton. Courtney's husband."

"Ohmigod!" says Morgan, taking Josh's hand and giggling with relief. "Wow! You're so good at that!"

"Years of practice," says Josh with a bad-boy shrug he perfected behind the bar.

"Are you, like, an actor too?" she croons.

"Nope," he says, flashing his hottest smile at her. "Just a writer."

"Writers are *so* sexy." Reagan grins at my husband, her eyes essentially undressing him. "Cute *and* talented? Whew! Too bad you're married."

"Only just," says Josh with an indulgent chuckle.

He's *flirting* with them. *Flirting.* And he *knows* how much I hate it.

"Lucky you got there first, Courts," says Reagan, still eye-fucking my spouse.

"Um. Yeah. I did," I say, stepping forward to clasp his hand.

"So, did you go to Tisch?" asks Reagan, licking her lips and completely ignoring me. "My niece went there."

"Really?" asks Josh. "Is she a redhead like you?"

"Mm-hm," hums Reagan, arching her back so her breasts are more prominent. "But hers is fake. I'm all natural...*everywhere.*"

Well, that's about enough of that.

"Thanks, Reagan," I say, "for that incredibly inappropriate visual."

"You had us going there, Dalton," says Bennett, stepping around the coffee table to stand beside Reagan. His face is hard, though. Not amused at all.

The sliding door to the deck opens and two more guys walk into the living room, whom I immediately identify as Stockard Chase and Harris DeFoe, both of whom attended King Low-Heywood Thomas prep school with me, Morgan and Bennett.

"Stock!" I say.

"Courtney Jane Salinger," he says, crossing the room to hug me. "Fuck. It's been a while."

I've always liked Stock Chase. With his bright red hair and emerald green eyes, he wasn't exactly my type physically, but we had a lot of classes together and he was always a solidly good guy.

I lean back and grin at him. "It's good to see you."

"Yeah," he says, his voice thoughtful. "You too. Really good."

"I'm Court's husband," says Josh, reaching around me to offer his free hand to Stock.

"Husband?" Stock looks completely confused for a second, then releases me to shake Josh's hand. "Stockard Chase."

"Josh Dalton."

"Good to meet you."

"Likewise."

"When did this happen?" asks Stock, looking back and forth from me to Josh, his eyes finally resting on mine.

"June," I say.

"Ah…" he says, his smile fading a little before he forces it back. "Recently. That's—that's great, Courtney. Congratulations."

"Thanks," says Josh, draping an arm over my shoulders and pulling me closer.

"Thanks," I say, still looking up at him.

For just a moment—just a millisecond, really—I wonder about the expression in Stock's eyes. We never dated. We were never, ever a "thing," even for a night. But I think I just caught a look of ever-so-subtle longing. That's what it felt like. That's what it kind of looked like too.

Does Stockard Chase have a thing for me? I quickly search my mind, remembering the many times we partied together. I always felt comfortable with him. It wasn't unusual for us to end up together at the end of the night, sitting side by side on loungers by the pool and staring up at the stars. But he never made a move on me and I never made one on him. We never even kissed.

I'm wrong. I must be wrong.

"Oh my God, you guys! We have to get out of here!"

yells Dina, who's standing in the double doorway to the great room. "I just got a text from Kyra. Beacon is *hopping* tonight!"

"I'm ready!" says Reagan.

"Me too!" Morgan takes out her phone, glancing around the room for a second. "We're...eight peeps. I'll get one Uber. Dee, you get the other one?"

"Def," says Dina. "Court, you want to go freshen up?"

"Yeah," I say. "Sure."

"You know where to go," says Dina. "Third bedroom on the left. You and Josh get the far bed."

"Perfect," I say, ducking under Josh's arm and heading for the stairs. He's brought our bags inside, and I grab mine. When we've reached the top of the stairs, I say, "That was *quite* a performance."

"Which part? Midwestern hick or flirty bartender?"

"Both were first rate," I snipe.

"Well, now, that doesn't sound like a compliment," he says.

"It wasn't."

"Aw," he says. "Too bad. It was all for you."

I get to the bedroom and open the door, stepping into the room and waiting for him to join me before closing the door. "I *said* I was sorry. I didn't mean it when I said that."

"Except," he says, "I think you did."

"Did *you* mean it? When you called me a 'spoiled brat'?"

He nods. "Yep. Pretty much I did."

I stare at him, hurt by this assessment.

I know where I'm from. I know that the per capita

income of a single person in Greenwich, Connecticut, is $670,000. I know that my parents' house is worth a cool fifteen million. I know I went to one of the finest prep schools on the east coast and I know that I had everything money could buy: horses, a tennis court, country club membership, New York apartment, Parisian weekends, Birkin bags, Manolo heels—you name it. Sure, I had it all.

But damn it to hell and back, I have done my very best *not* to live my adult life as a spoiled rich-bitch. I have tried to be a good person, a kind person, and most of all, a self-aware person. I have tried my best to leave my wealthy, entitled childhood in the past, and make my own way, living by my own means.

And okay, maybe I was being impatient in the car. Maybe I was even being downright bitchy about the traffic and being late to meet my friends, but it's too easy to call me a spoiled brat because of where I come from. It's not fair. It's not...fucking...fair.

I drop my bag on our bed, then turn to face my husband, hands on my hips, feeling absolutely furious.

"And that's who I am now, right?"

He looks at me from across the room. "Huh?"

"A spoiled brat! A rich bitch! That's who I am to you now, right?"

"That's how you were *acting*." He throws his bag on the floor and puts his hands on his hips, his eyes furious. "You made me feel like total shit, Courtney!"

"Well, that's how I feel now!" I shout, breathing so hard and so fast my shoulders are practically brushing my ears. "Don't...Don't..."

"Don't what?" he asks, advancing toward me.

"Don't think of me like that! Please!"

His face is angry and the muscles on his forearms are flexed and taut. "Then don't act like that!"

"I'm not...I'm not like them. I've tried...I mean, I don't want..." My eyes are burning and I'm so mad at him, but I'm even more sorry for what I said about him.

He purses his lips, then says in a gentler voice, "I've never seen you behave like that before."

I realize that the only way to explain where my attitude came from is to finally say the words that have been perched on my tongue since last weekend, "You have to understand...I've never had *anyone* tell me how I could spend my money. Never."

He stares at me for a second, then nods slowly. "Okay. I get that."

"It *really* bothered me."

"I can see how it might."

"I don't know how to get on the same page with you about this, but it's driving me crazy."

He takes a deep breath, then sighs. "You're not single anymore. Neither of us is. We're married. We're a unit, Court. A team. We're responsible for each other."

"I understand that in theory, but—"

"What if something happens to your job?" he asks, his voice serious and firm. "What if there are lay-offs at your company? Another financial depression? What if—I don't know—what if something happens, God forbid, and you can't work anymore?"

I stare at him, processing his words, part of me shocked by what he's saying. I don't think about doomsday stuff like this. I never really have.

"I'll get another job," I say.

"What if you can't find one right away?"

"It's fine."

"Really? How much money have you saved?"

"If we need money, we'll just tap into my…"

My voice trails off into silence as I look up at him.

Oh my God.

"Your trust?" he asks softly.

And that's when I get it—when I *finally* get it.

I have almost nothing in savings. I've never *needed* savings because I've always had my trust. He's right. I don't have any savings independent of my family. I have my income and that's it.

"If something happens to my job," I say gently, "you're worried that you won't be able to support us."

"I have nothing. No savings, Court. I suspected you didn't either, because your trust was always your back-up." He closes the distance between us, looking down at me, his eyes more tender and loving than I deserve. "We have nothing saved."

"You're worried?" I ask him, stepping close enough that my chest grazes his.

"Yeah. Of course," he says with a little shrug. "I'm worried I won't be able to take care of you if something happens."

There's a knock at the door and Dina opens it, sticking her head into the room. "Are you guys ready? *Andale!*"

"We're not coming," I whisper, staring deeply into my husband's eyes.

"But…" she starts. She must sense the tension in the room and quickly shifts gears. "Yeah. Umm…okay. Catch you two in the morning."

The door closes behind her and a second later I'm in Josh's arms.

"I'm sorry," he breathes against my hair. "I'm sorry I said you were a spoiled brat. I didn't mean it. You're kind and smart and amazing…you're *everything* to me, Court."

"I was such a bitch to you! I deserved it," I say, leaning back to look up into his eyes. "I'm sorry too. I never want you to feel "less-than" when you're my everything."

He cups my face like I'm precious to him, like, maybe, he's fallen in love with me, and my heart fills with so much emotion, so much gratitude and love for him, I can barely contain it.

"I just want us to be responsible."

"We will be. We can start saving," I say. "I'll open a savings account for us on Monday."

He strokes my cheek. "That's my girl."

I reach for his hand and move it to my shirt, pressing it over my heart. "Now, you listen to me, Josh from Minnetonka. My heart is yours. And I want you *exactly* the way you are. Got it?"

He's already smiling at me, but he chuckles softly. "Sure?"

"Ya betcha," I say back, wrapping my arms around his neck and rising up on my tiptoes to kiss him.

CHAPTER 6
• EXES •

"A good rule of thumb about exes is that if you're not sharing your communication with an ex openly with your spouse, it's probably not a good idea. Lurking on your ex's Facebook page while your wife's working late? Don't. Sending texts to your ex-boyfriend that your spouse doesn't know about? Don't, again."
--Dr. Sydney Morningstar

<u>Josh</u>

"Hey, babe, you've got the drinks handled?" she asks me.

Courtney's in the shower while I'm flossing my teeth at the sink.

"Uh-huh. Wholesale discount from Lulu," I say. "Two cases of white, two of red, and four of beer."

"In cans or bottles?" she asks.

"Cans. Cheaper."

"Cool," she says. "I've got food handled. Catered trays should get here by five."

"What time will you be home?"

On Fridays, my wife sometimes surprises me by walking in the door at two or three o'clock, which is always awesome, because we act all surprised and treat it like the perfect excuse to jump each other. I'm like Pavlov's dog every Friday afternoon now, hoping to hear her key in the lock.

"Hard to say," she says, pushing the curtain aside and peeking at me with drops of water glistening on her eyelashes. "Maybe early. If I can swing it."

My cock hardens at the thought, and as she pulls the curtain shut, I unfasten the towel from around my waist and step inside the steaming shower. I'm quiet, though, and she's leaning back, rinsing her hair with her eyes closed, so she doesn't realize I've joined her until my hands are massaging her slippery breasts.

She doesn't open her eyes, but she sighs, low and soft, her slick lips tilting up in a smile as she continues to lean her head back in the stream of hot water. Her breasts are full and gorgeous, the areolas light pink and the already-erect nipples a deeper rose. I suck one into my mouth, lapping at the warm water, then pursing my lips around the tightening bud of flesh. Skimming my lips across her chest, I lick the water off her other nipple, my thumb and forefinger gently squeezing the former until she moans, covering my hands with hers.

Opening her eyes, she puts her hands on my shoulders and pushes me back to the built-in bench at the back of the shower.

"Sit," she says, slowly lowering herself to her knees before me.

My cock is hard and twitching, and my breath is shallow with anticipation.

Fisting me at the base of my erection, she leans forward and slides her beautiful lips over the swollen head of my cock, her head bobbing as she sucks me in, then lets me go. I wind her hair around my hand, not to force her, but to keep it out of her way as she takes me deeper and deeper into her mouth until I'm groaning, the guttural sounds bouncing off the tiled walls.

I cup her cheeks and force her head up until her eyes meet mine. "I want you."

"Always," she says, bracing her hands on my knees and standing up.

Smiling at me, she turns around, then carefully lowers herself onto my stiff, wet cock, with her back to my front. I reach forward, both to keep her from falling forward as I thrust up and forward, but also to cup her breasts in my hands as I make love to her. Her hands land on my thighs, her fingernails biting into my skin as my thrusts get deeper and faster.

My balls tighten and clench, and I know I'm going to come any second, but I try to hold out, because when Courtney comes in this position, she rides out her orgasm with the back of her head on my shoulder. *Come on, baby*, I think, rolling one nipple between my fingers as my other hand slips down her stomach to finger her clit. Rubbing it with my middle finger in broad strokes while I continue to pump my cock into her, I finally feel the weight of her head fall back onto my shoulder, followed by her whimpers of pleasure. Once I know she's satisfied, I let go, coming inside of her while the walls of her pussy milk every drop of my cum.

I hold onto her tightly as the last shudders rock my

body, my arms around her waist, the back of her head still resting on my shoulder.

I don't want to let her go. I never ever want to let her go.

"Let's sit here all day," I suggest, panting between my words.

"With your dick inside of me and the shower running? We'll prune."

Sometimes she uses dirty words before, during, or after we fuck, and it's so unexpected and hot and *unexpectedly hot*, it makes my recently-sated cock twitch within her body.

"I'm definitely *not* pruning," I point out.

"What'll we say when our guests show up tonight?" she asks. "We're in here, guys!"

I laugh, rolling my head to the side to kiss her cheek. "Yeah. I guess it wouldn't work."

Pushing off from my lap, she stands up, and I sit up, staring at the junction of her thighs where a stream of my cum slides down her leg. Call it a primal instinct, but it makes my heart beat faster. Part of me is still inside of her. She's mine. She belongs to me.

"Fuck, my wife is hot."

"Well, now she's dirty too," she replies, reaching for the shower nozzle and spraying off her pussy and legs. She grins at me over her shoulder. "That's your cue to get out of here. I need to be at the office in thirty minutes and you're making me late."

"Yeah, yeah. I'm going."

I've already taken a morning run, so after getting

dressed and having a quick breakfast with Courtney, I take my laptop up to the roof deck and sit in the morning sun to do a little work.

My play, *Miss Gibbs Will See You Now*, needs to be sent to the judges at Simi Frederick's festival no later than September 1st, which means I only have three weeks to perfect it. Over the next two weeks I've booked studio time at the New Dramatists for some back to back run-throughs, and then I'll have a few days left for final tweaks and edits before the due date.

It's hard for me, as an artist, to be objective about my work, but I think it's a good classical-style play. And if it does well in the Emerging Playwrights competition, I could see it staged at Lincoln Center.

Today, in preparation for Monday's run-through with acting students, I'm re-reading the entire play from front to back, and I'm hoping every word feels perfect.

Set in the 1890s, *Miss Gibbs Will See You Now* is the story of a young, unhappily married woman who travels from southern Staten Island to midtown Manhattan one morning to try to sell her manuscript to Mr. Gordon Gibbs, one of the most prominent publishers in New York. The reason she's chosen Gibbs & Sons is because—in my fictional world—that particular publishing house has previously published works by Edith Wharton and Kate Chopin. My heroine, Pippa Forrester, who has married a tugboat captain and feels shackled to her duties and obligations as a wife, is hopeful they might consider publishing her novel as well.

When she arrives at the office building without an appointment, Mr. Gibbs is not available to see the young author, but his daughter, respected short story editor, Miss Eliza Gibbs, has a cancelation in her day and agrees to hear Pippa's pitch.

When the receptionist gestures to Pippa and says, "Miss Gibbs will see you now," Pippa feels her entire world turn on the tip of a needle, on the width of a hair. Suddenly, everything that seemed almost *im*possible is almost possible. As she stands up and makes her way to Miss Gibbs' office, the metaphorical glass above and around her shatters.

Later, as Pippa Forrester recounts the highlights of her life, including the days of her birth and marriage, she regards that single moment as the most important of her life, and the rest of the play shows the effects of that liberation on the course of her middle-class life.

By the time I finish reading several hours later, I'm tired and hungry, and my arms are sunburned, but I am more positive than ever that my play could be a contender for first place. I can already imagine the sets and costuming, the woman I imagine as Pippa, not so unlike my own beautiful wife: blonde and blue-eyed, from a genteel family, but married to someone beneath her in both social status and wealth. In Pippa's case, it leads to unhappiness.

I check the time and realize that Courtney will be unhappy if I don't get off my ass and go to Tidewaters for the ice, wine, and beer. I need to start setting up everything for our first jointly-hosted party tonight.

After last weekend in the Hamptons—which, by the

way, was much better after we had make-up sex all over the house before her friends returned home on Friday night—I have to admit I'm a little worried about mixing our friend-groups. Courtney's friends are wealthy and entitled. Mine are poor and struggling. Hers are living in doorman high rises, while mine are gratefully sharing shoeboxes. Hers take almost everything for granted, while mine will be shocked by the sheer excess of our cocktail party, which includes six cases of alcohol with *catered* cheese and cracker platters.

But even mixing our wildly different friends isn't what has me the most rattled.

It's Sam.

It's the fact that I haven't seen Sam since she sent me those texts, and she's coming tonight.

And maybe even more than that, it's the fact that I never shared those texts with Courtney.

As I walk back from Tidewaters pushing a borrowed hand truck loaded with cardboard boxes of alcohol, I ask myself why I never showed the texts to Courtney and a million reasons surface.

Because my wife has a jealous streak and I didn't want to make her jealous over a girl about whom I have zero romantic feelings or interest…Because I got those messages on the last day of our honeymoon when our return to New York was imminent and we had no idea what to expect. I didn't think she needed the pile-on of knowing her husband's ex-girlfriend was pursuing him…Because I'm a well-established chickenshit when it comes to confrontation with women. I hate it with my mother. I loathed it with Sam.

And when Courtney and I are at odds, I swear to God, it feels so bad, I can barely breathe.

As I load the beer and white wine into the fridge and set up the red wine on the kitchen counter, a low-grade panic starts turning over my stomach. Shit. I should have told Courtney about the texts. Or at the very least, I shouldn't have invited Sam tonight. If I had cut off all contact with her, my fears for tonight wouldn't be an issue. Maybe I should uninvite her? Or—

My cell phone buzzes and I take it out of my back pocket.

The one afternoon I want to be home early, and Joel needs me to stay late. Have I mentioned how much I hate my boss?

Yep. She's mentioned what an asshole he is.

The night she came home from Japan, after we sorted out my going back to work behind her back, she told me that he hit on her a couple of times in Tokyo and again on the car ride from Newark to New York. I offered to go to her office and talk to him or pick her up after work some evening and introduce myself as her husband, but she declined. She wanted to deal with it herself, and I promised to respect her decision.

But it makes me feel bad that she told me about her boss hitting on her, and I didn't tell her about Sam hitting on me. I'm tempted to say something now, but I know she's nervous about tonight too, and I really don't want to make a mountain out of a molehill. Sam said she was "going through a thing" and wanted the texts to be "water under the bridge." God, I just hope she meant that and doesn't pull anything tonight.

If he touches you again, I'm visiting him with a baseball bat.

Not necessary. He hasn't bothered me since Japan. How's the party planning coming along?

Beer and white wine are chilling. Red is set up on the counter. And guess what! Miss Gibbs is *almost* ready for your eyes.

You mean it? she asks, with a shocked-face emoji. *I can FINALLY read your baby?*

I've got run-throughs this week and next, and then a little tweaking. But, soon!

YAY! she types back. *Hey! Should we go away? Get out of town and go to a B&B where I can read in peace?* A good twenty seconds go by before she adds: *Somewhere affordable, of course.*

She does this a lot—suggests something fun, and then makes sure I know that she isn't trying to subvert our goals to save and live within our means. Honestly, it means a lot to me.

It also makes me more amenable to her suggestions.

That sounds amazing, I say. *You're so thoughtful, babe.*

She sends back a happy face, then asks if she should send over Dina a little early to help set up.

I don't actually need Dina's help—I'll set the catering platters on the coffee table in the living room when they're delivered, and I'm perfectly able to choose some music and answer the door. That said, however, I like Dina and I didn't feel like I got to visit with her much last weekend at *Chez Douche.*

When we first arrived at the house in the Hamptons, Dina came out to the car to say hello while Courtney went inside with two other girls. I told Dina that Courtney had been throwing around attitude like *mardi gras* beads on Bourbon Street, and she countered that Courtney was the first of their crew to get married. She asked me to try to see it from Courtney's point of view—introducing her husband to old friends for the first time, knowing full and well how predatory the girls would be and how douche-y the guys would be. It didn't make me feel better, per se, but it did get me out of the car.

Sure, I say. *Why not? Send her over.*

You know, she writes back. *Dina is the only woman in the whole world that I trust alone with you.*

She adds a smiley face to this statement to soften her words, but it feels like a harbinger of doom, and that low-grade panic inside of me triples in intensity.

You're the only woman for me, I type. *You know that, right? No matter what, it's you and me.*

I know, she answers. *#TeamDalton! And for the record, I trust you, Josh. You've never given me a reason not to.*

"Fuck," I whisper, but now isn't the time to come clean about Sam's texts. It's just not. It'll just make trouble where none—*probably, hopefully, God willing*—exists.

#TeamDalton, baby. See you later, I answer, praying that everything goes smoothly tonight.

***

Courtney

Joel Morris hasn't hit on me since the car ride from Newark Airport in June, but he's also excluded me from several important international projects since that trip.

My gut feeling is that he's punishing me for refusing his advances, but God! I'm married. And even if I *wasn't* married, I *still* wouldn't be interested.

However, keeping my job is more important than ever. Without it, Josh's and my income would drop by about seventy-five percent, and although we're determined to be more aggressive about savings, it's going to be a few months before we have a substantial "rainy-day" nest egg established.

So, when Joel asked me to stay late tonight for a meeting, I couldn't say no. But my heart feels heavy as I leave my office and walk over to his. The only plus is that I'll get to say hi to Dina and ask her to head to my place a little early to greet our mutual friends in case things with Joel run late.

She greets me with a big smile, looking as beautiful as ever in a hot pink silk blouse and cream-colored pencil skirt.

"Courts!"

"Hey, Dee," I say, trudging into the anteroom where Dina answers Joel's phone and receives his visitors. I lean my elbows on her desk. "I can't believe I have to stay late tonight."

"Yeah, well, Corbin and Benson passed up this project. You're the third pick. I think you should make the most of it," she says, giving me a "suck-it-up" look.

"So, he *is* passing me over lately." I flick a look at his office door. "I knew it."

"Did something happen?"

"I just don't want to be the next Mrs. Morris," I say.

"Especially since I'm already the first Mrs. Dalton."

"Ahhhh," hums Dina. "He's been hitting on you. Naughty Joel."

"You know how he is."

"Actually, I don't. Not first-hand anyway. I've heard the stories, of course...but, he doesn't go after brown-skinned girls."

"I should have known he was a racist too."

Dina chuckles. "I'd be offended if I was interested, but I'm not. *At all.* It keeps things very professional between us which is exactly how I want it."

"Hey," I say, "just in case things go late here, will you go to my place a little early? Some of the Hamptons' crew is stopping by. It'll go smoother if you're there to greet them."

"Of course."

"I know we haven't had a lot of time to catch up since I got back from my honeymoon...but I miss you."

"You came out to the Hamptons last week," she points out.

"Yeah, but we barely got any one on one time. How about a pedi soon?"

"Next weekend?"

I remember my plan to go away to a B&B with Josh. "I can't. The weekend after?"

"I'm in East Hampton for all of August, right up until Labor Day."

"Some evening after work?" I ask.

"Can you *bear* to pull yourself away from your hot husband?" asks Dina with a hint of attitude, giving me side-eyes.

I grimace. "I guess I haven't been around much."

"You've pretty much ghosted everyone," she agrees, but a small smile plays on the corners of her mouth. "But I get it. You're newlyweds. You're in love. You're probably having sex on every surface of your apartment." She cringes. "Speaking of which...did your housekeeper come this morning?"

I stick out my tongue at her and she laughs at me.

"Nah. I'm happy for you," she says. "Really. Josh is a great guy. I love it that you guys got together."

"He is," I agree, "though no one's said the "L" word yet."

"Huh?"

"You said we're "newlyweds" and "in love." But neither of us has said it yet."

"Really?" she asks, looking genuinely surprised.

"No. Not yet. Why? What?"

"Well, I mean, I'm only looking at you two from the outside, but I can't remember the last time I saw two people who looked more in love. I'm expecting you to walk in here any day now and tell me you're planning for maternity leave."

Thud. My heart.

I open my mouth to say something, but nothing comes out; the lump in my throat won't let me speak. I look down at the desktop, glancing at my wedding rings and telling myself absolutely, positively not to cry.

"Courts? Hey. What'd I say?"

I look up and clear my throat. "He's not…I mean, he's not sure he wants kids."

"What? What do you mean?"

"I brought it up on our honeymoon—just in passing. You know, like, "one day maybe we'll have kids," or something like that, and he totally freaked. And it came up one other time and he—I don't know—he froze. He shut down. He changed the subject."

"He doesn't *want* kids?"

She says this like it's totally unbelievable.

"Not now. Maybe not ever."

"How do you feel about that?" She gives me a sympathetic look. "You don't need to answer. Your face says it all." She reaches for my hand and covers it with hers. "What are you going to do?"

"I don't know," I whisper. "Hope he'll change his mind?"

"That's really your only option," she says. "It's not like compromising on where you spend Christmas. It's all or nothing when it comes to kids."

"I know."

"Hey," she says, "maybe he'll change his mind. You never know."

"Maybe." I gulp over the lump in my throat and take a deep breath. "It's early days."

"Definitely," she says, smiling at me and patting my hand just before her intercom beeps. "Is Ms. Salinger here?"

"You mean Ms. Dalton? Yes, sir."

"Send her in, please," he grumbles.

"Right away, sir." She looks up at me and winces. "Time to face the music."

I gather my file folders against my chest like armor and give her a brave smile. "Catch you later."

***

It's almost nine o'clock by the time I leave the office to head home.

When I step out of my building onto the sidewalk, I'm beyond relieved to be finished with work for this week and especially grateful to be away from Joel for a couple of days.

Tonight's meeting was a mixed bag of business, innuendo, and thinly-veiled threats, the worst of which was Joel letting me know that if my attitude didn't "improve," I could kiss a partnership goodbye.

"My attitude is the same as it's ever been," I told him in as level a voice as I could manage.

"Not true," he answered. "You don't seem as willing to do anything for the team."

"I was never willing to do *anything*."

"Right there!" he exclaimed, slapping his palm on his desk. "That's the very sort of snarky comment that makes a workplace feel hostile, Courtney."

"Hostile?" I cried. "If anyone's made this workplace uncomfortable, Joel, it's you. I don't know if my father told you, but since we last talked, I'm married."

"Yes, I heard." His eyes narrowed. "To the playwright?"

"Yes."

His face had gradually relaxed from surprised to smug,

and he finally said, "It won't last."

"I hope you're wrong," I answered, then redirected the conversation, as I already had several times before. "Shall we take a look at the Danish numbers again?"

Again and again I tried to keep us focused on work, but Joel jockeyed back and forth between petulant and contentious. He ended the meeting abruptly, telling me to do a workup on the market trends for various Scandinavian banks and have it on his desk Monday morning. So, great. Now I have to work this weekend too.

As I walk home, I think about contacting Human Resources and speaking to them about Joel's behavior, but I know it won't really do any good. He owns the company—it's been in his family forever. The best I could hope for is overcompensation for my "troubles" and a decent severance package, no doubt with a nondisclosure agreement forbidding me to discuss my employment at DeWitt, Morris & Jones. I could live with all of that...but I'd leave with my reputation in shreds. Joel would crucify me to all of his cronies so that once I set up my own shop, I'd surely be blackballed by the Wall Street elite.

"This is such bullshit," I mutter, crossing my arms over my chest.

"I agree," says a voice from beside me. "Late to her own party."

My head jerks up and I'm surprised to find Stockard Chase walking beside me. My face blooms into a smile of recognition. "Hey!"

"Hey!" he answers.

"Where'd you come from?"

He grins. "A few doors down from you. Saw you leave and caught up."

"No Hamptons this weekend?"

"Nah," he says. "I was only there at Morgan's invitation."

"Are you two…?"

"Me and Morgan?" He fake shudders. "No. No, thanks."

"She's gorgeous!" I say. "Not your type?"

He follows me into my building, and we head for the elevator. "I prefer blondes."

My skin prickles, but I shake it off.

As the elevator doors close, he turns to me. "I was really surprised about your marriage."

"Yeah," I say, crossing my arms over my chest. "Everything happened quickly."

He takes a deep breath. "So quickly I feel like I didn't get a chance."

"For what?"

He shrugs. "For you."

I avert my eyes, looking up at the glowing numbers over the door and wishing they'd go faster.

"I don't mean to make you uncomfortable," he says softly.

"No. It's okay. I'm fine. It's just that I'm married now," I say. "I—I chose Josh. We're together. I…"

"Do you love him?"

Yes. But I'm not going to tell Stock before I tell Josh.

"He's my husband," I say firmly. I tilt my head to the side and offer a small smile. "Where's this coming from? We were always *friends*, Stock. Nothing more."

"Maybe sometimes you don't know what you want until you can't have it anymore."

"How about we try to find you someone else tonight, huh?"

Mercifully, the elevator dings. But as we step into the hallway, he takes my arm. "Listen, if things don't work out the way you want them to…or if you just need to talk, or—"

"Thanks, Stock, but we're doing good." I pull my arm away. "Come on. Let's get you a drink."

The music's loud and my apartment feels packed, though there are only about twenty people here. I put my briefcase and purse in the front hall closet, then make my way down the hallway to the living room. Saying "hello" to various friends who've stopped by, I'm looking for Josh, and when I finally see him, he's on the far side of the room, speaking to a petite, dark-haired woman by the windows.

I grab two glasses of wine from the kitchen counter and make my way to his side. His eyes catch mine as I'm crossing the room, and he smiles, but it's not a carefree expression. It's shadowed by another emotion I can't quite pinpoint. Discomfort? Worry? Hmm.

"You're here," he says, pulling me against his side and kissing my cheek. "I missed you."

"Joel kept me late."

"Do I need to kick his ass?" he asks me.

"Maybe," I answer. "I'll let you know."

I step out of his embrace and offer him one of the wineglasses. "Need a refill?"

As he takes it, a voice from behind me says,

"Josh doesn't drink wine."

I turn to the woman he was talking to and stiffen a little when I recognize her as Samantha—Sammy—Josh's ex-girlfriend. I met her very briefly in the spring when Josh took me to her play at the Mitzi Newhouse Theater.

"You're Sam," I say, holding out my free hand. "Hi. I'm Courtney."

"I know who you are." Her smile is brittle as she reaches over me to take the wineglass from Josh's hand.

"Josh doesn't drink wine," she repeats, placing the offending glass on the windowsill. "He's allergic to the tannins."

Now that she's mentioned it, I realize that I've never seen Josh drinking wine. Beer's his beverage of choice. But I had no idea that he was allergic.

"I didn't know that," I say, glancing at Josh.

He shrugs. "I can drink it now and then."

"Sure, but then you break out," says Sam, flashing a warm, teasing smile at her ex. "Remember that time we went to the Berkshires? You were up all night with hives, poor baby."

Josh clears his throat, giving me a sheepish smile. "It wasn't that bad—"

"Yes, it was!" Sam insists. "Don't you remember? It got so bad, I made you strip so I could rub ice cubes all over your back."

"Well," I say, feeling my cheeks flush as my mind creates a mental image of my husband naked with his ex, "I'll have to remember that if it ever happens again." Eager to change the subject, I say, "I saw your play in the spring."

Her grin is frosty. "Oh, right. Josh brought you along...as a friend."

She's clearly trying to lay down some kind of gauntlet, but I'm not having it. Josh is mine. My man. My husband. And no ex-girlfriend is going to walk into my home and make a play for him. *Not* happening.

"Friendship's a perfect basis for marriage, don't you think?" I ask her.

Josh puts an arm around my waist and pulls me back against his chest. "It worked for us."

"Frankly, I think *love* is the only recipe for marriage." Sam's icy expression turns into a snarky smirk as she says, "Hey! Didn't I hear something about your marriage being *arranged*? Almost like a business deal?"

I'm stunned by her meanness, scrambling to think of what to say in response, when my husband's voice rumbles softly beside my ear.

"I love her," he says.

"What?" demands Sam, blinking at Josh.

"You said that love is the only recipe for marriage," he says. His arm tightens around me. "I agree. I'm in love with Courtney. I love her."

Tears spring to my eyes and I cover Josh's hand with my free one, tilting my head back so that he can kiss me.

When I fantasized about Josh telling me that he loved

me, I imagined it would happen while we were making love, or over dinner at a romantic restaurant. My hypothetical declarations never included a showdown between me and Josh's ex. But suddenly *now* is the *perfect* time, the *best* time, and as our kiss deepens, I turn in his arms, giving my heart to my husband and my back to Sam. I wrap my arms around his neck and show him, with my body, with my ardor, how much his sweet words mean to me.

Gradually, I realize that people are clapping and hooting, and I break off this intimate moment with my husband to find that most of the room is looking at us with glasses raised.

"Congratulations to the happy couple!" exclaims Dina, who has cut the music and is standing on the coffee table. "To my good friends, Mr. and Mrs. Joshua Dalton! May you have a lifetime of kisses as sizzling as that one!"

My face is a scorching pink as everyone clinks their glasses together and then Dina jumps down and turns the music back up. When I look at Sam over my shoulder, her eyes are dark slits. She raises them to Josh.

"Delete my texts, would you? I've changed my mind. In fact, I'm embarrassed I ever sent them."

She slides away from us, heading for the kitchen.

I turn to Josh. "Texts?"

His jaw flexes for a moment. "I love you."

"I know. I heard," I say, tilting my head to the side. "What texts?"

"Come with me."

He takes my hand and we weave in and out of various

friend groupings, saying brief hellos, as he leads me down the back hallway to our bedroom. After he closes the door, we sit down on the edge of the bed and he takes his phone out of his back pocket, handing it to me. I take it without a word and click on the text icon, then scroll down for messages from Sam.

"Where do I start?"

"The last day of our honeymoon."

My eyes whip up to catch his in the dim light. "You've been texting her since then?"

"It's not what you think," he says. "Just read."

I scroll up, over a recent conversation, and stopping at the first of six very long messages which it appears he received during our time in Scotland.

Sam pours her heart out, telling Josh that she still loves him and asking for another chance. She also mentions that she'd never cheat on him "again," and says that she doesn't care if he's married; she insists that they need to talk.

I can't lie. I'm shaken by what I read. I'm uncomfortable that another woman has feelings this strong for my husband.

"Did you talk to her?"

"Not when I got these."

"What did you do?"

He shrugs. "Ignored them."

The part of me who was recently single feels a moment of sympathy for Sam, but it's quickly overshadowed by an overwhelming sense of relief that he didn't engage with her.

"Why didn't you tell me?"

"I should have," he says, putting an arm around my shoulders. "But at the same time I got Sam's texts, you heard from your father. You were so upset. I didn't want to make things worse for you."

It's sweet, but this has been a pattern in our marriage—Josh and I keeping things from each other because we're worried about our spouse's reaction or we don't want to overwhelm each other—and I feel strongly that we need to correct it. He needs to know he can talk to me, and vice versa. About anything.

"I'm not porcelain, Josh."

"I know that now. I know how strong you are."

I look down at the messages again. "You never wrote back to her."

He shakes his head. "Nope. Not until she wrote again last week asking about tonight."

"And you invited her? I mean, she *had* just declared her undying love."

"Yeah, I know. But she said it was all "water under the bridge" and asked if we could move on."

"And you believed her? After those texts?"

He nods. "I wanted to believe her. We were friends for a long time. We have a lot of friends in common. We both workshop our plays at the New Dramatists. I was hoping—I don't know—that maybe we could go back to friends. I guess that was a stupid thing to hope."

"Is this why you've been working from home so much?" I ask. I'd noticed that he didn't go to the New Dramatists much anymore, but I didn't see anything wrong with him working here. "To avoid her?"

He nods again. "Yeah."

"So…you never wrote back, and you've been avoiding her."

"Yeah. Pretty much."

"Then why do you look so guilty?" I ask with a soft chuckle as I place a palm gently against his cheek.

"Because I should have told you. I hate it that I kept the texts a secret from you. I don't want to have any secrets from you. Not now. Not ever."

"I want that too." I place his phone behind us on the bed and cup his other cheek, looking deeply into his eyes. "I love you."

His eyebrows furrow and he groans softly, leaning forward to kiss me. It's a tender kiss, filled with joy and relief and something else that makes me wonder if—despite the fact that he doesn't want children like I do—our marriage to each other can be enough, and I say a silent prayer that it is.

When I lean back his eyes are glistening. "You love me?"

"I love you," I whisper.

"You forgive me for keeping the texts a secret?"

"I forgive you," I answer. "And I trust you, Josh. Completely. No more jealousy. I promise."

"You want to get rid of all these people and fuck in the shower?" he asks, grinning at me.

"Hey, guys!" I call into the quiet darkness of our bedroom. "We're in here!"

He chuckles, caressing my cheek with his hand. "I guess

that's not such a hot idea, huh?"

"It's hot alright, but I think we should save it for later."

I kiss his palm, then take his hand, standing up and pulling him up with me. "Back to the party, Mr. Dalton?"

"Back to the party, Mrs. Dalton," he says, leaning down to kiss me once more before we head back to our guests, hand in hand, Team Dalton, together.

CHAPTER 7

• TRUST •

"Ask your partner to share the most intimate parts of themselves with you. Issue an invitation that says: "You are welcome here with me. All parts of you are loved by me." Acceptance is the key to trust."
--Dr. Sydney Morningstar

<u>Josh</u>

When Courtney finds out that Billy Joel's former summer house on the Hudson River has been renovated into a B&B, she calls to see if they have an available room for Saturday night. Lucky for us, they've had a last-minute cancellation, so we book a room and head north in mid-August for a mini-break upstate.

My run-throughs of *Miss Gibbs Will See You Now* at the New Dramatists were amazing, and I'm more confident than ever that I could win Simi Frederick's competition. In fact, after Courtney reads the play this weekend, I'll be sending it off with fingers crossed.

We drive up the eastern banks of the Hudson to the Bear Mountain Bridge in Montgomery, New York, where we cross over. From there, it's only three miles north to our B&B, Overlook on the Hudson. It's a surprisingly modest-sized house, but the innkeepers are gracious and warm, directing us to our room and leaving us to get settled.

I put her floral duffel bag on top of a bureau, and my backpack beside it.

"Did you bring up my purse?" she asks.

"No. I didn't see it."

"Huh. It must still be in the car. I'll grab it later," she says, crossing the room to look out the window. "Oh my God! It's so beautiful!"

Standing behind her, I check out the view, and I have to agree that it's pretty spectacular.

One of the reasons Courtney was drawn to this particular inn is that they have an outdoor pool and patio with grand, sweeping views of the Hudson. With the sun shining on the sparkling water in the aqua blue pool and the dark river beyond, it's absolutely gorgeous.

That said, I send a fleeting glance at the giant, king-sized bed.

"Come on over here, woman," I say, throwing my T-shirt on the floor and lying back on the plush comforter.

She climbs on top of me, fully clothed—*more's the pity*—straddling my waist. Leaning down, she gives me a super-quick kiss on the lips. "Nope. I want some fun in the sun."

I lean up on my elbows. "But I love you and you're so hot and I want to fuck."

"Awww. And I love you and you're so hot...but I want to swim," she answers, climbing off of me with a giggle.

As usual, my wife gets her way, and ten minutes later, we're in the pool together, admiring the views of the Hudson River in our bathing suits.

"I love it here," says Courtney, propping her elbows on the side of the pool and staring out over the river to the rugged banks beyond. "You know, I've often thought about buying a house somewhere up here. For weekends. In the summer...at Christmas..."

"But you want to live full-time in the city, right?" I ask, coming up behind her and bracketing her inside of my arms, which I rest on either side of her elbows.

"I love the city," she says. "I mean, I spent my early childhood there and I've lived there since I finished grad school."

"I hear a "but"..."

She takes a deep breath, which expands her chest and pushes her against me.

"It doesn't matter," she finally says, but there's sadness—*such sadness*—in the words, they clutch at my heart.

"Hey, come on. What?"

"Nope." She leans forward, away from me as much as she can, and rests her chin on her hands.

It bothers me that she won't tell me what she's thinking. I don't want to push her, but I don't want her to be sad either. I want her to trust me with anything—with *everything*—going on in her head.

"Why won't you tell me?"

"Because you won't like it."

"Tell me anyway," I whisper near her ear.

She clears her throat and takes another deep breath. "When I think about having a house in the country where we spend summer weekends or Christmas vacation, I don't just see us there."

"Who else? Your parents?" Shit. Of course she's sad to be at odds with her parents, and frankly, I haven't been checking in with her enough about it. She's given up her relationship with them *and* her trust fund just to be with me. "Court, you know they're going to come around eventually, right?"

"Oh, yeah," she says, her voice, surprisingly, lightening up a little. "I know. I mean, I hope," she sighs. "But if they can't accept you, that's their problem. All I can do is be available for a loving, respectful relationship when they're ready to offer one."

Her answer is so sensible and accepting, I fear I haven't uncovered the reason for her sadness, and it's *really* starting to bother me.

"Is there anything else?" I ask, resting my chin on her shoulder. "Something's still bugging you. I know it."

"Josh...what do we do when we *feel* something that we're not sure the other person will like or accept?"

Huh. Maybe she doesn't like living in New York? Maybe she's trying to tell me she wants to move out to the country and using the example of weekends and holidays as a way to make me agree? Well, living in the Hudson Valley would be a change, for sure, but we could figure it out, right? Compromise.

"We trust each other with our truth, whatever it is," I tell her. "If this is yours, I want to know it, and even if I don't like it or agree with it, I will make room for discussing it. We can figure out anything together."

The commute would suck, I think, but if it really meant that much to her to move, we could make a timeline together, and maybe make it happen in a year or two.

"But what happens if we *don't* agree? If you *don't* like 'my truth'?" she asks.

"We'll keep talking. There's always compromise."

"Not with this," she murmurs, her voice soft and faraway.

"Tell me, baby," I insist.

She turns around in the water, facing me, her body still bracketed by mine.

"Don't be mad," she says.

"I won't be," I say. "I promise."

She scans my eyes desperately before whispering, "I—I want kids. At least one. I can't help it, Josh. I want to know we'll have a family someday."

"Wait. What?"

Her words blindside me, and I let go of the pool edge, stepping away from her.

"You said you wouldn't be mad," she says.

"I'm not...mad," I tell her. "But...I mean...I thought you were going to say you wanted to move." I run a hand through my wet hair. "We've talked about this already."

"No, we haven't," she says. "Not really. Twice I've brought it up and twice you've shot it down. We haven't *talked* about it at all."

I can't help the way my heart's beating faster, the way a vague and discomfiting panic is gripping me. I can't explain it, but it's happened both times Courtney's brought up having kids.

Honestly, I don't know why it scares me so much, but mostly I think it comes down to two things: one, loving my life the way it is, and two, not feeling ready. Kids change everything. Kids make you...old.

"Why are you so against it?" she asks.

"I'm not *against* it, like *fundamentally*," I say, "but I'm not ready. And I don't know when I'll be ready, so it's easier just to say it's not something I want right now."

"I don't think anyone's ever ready," she answers. "I think it's terrifying no matter what."

"Then forgive me for wanting to wait."

"Last time we talked, I asked if you wanted kids and you said that maybe you didn't."

"Right."

"Well...which is it? You don't want kids *now*? Or you don't want kids *ever*? I mean, can you imagine a time when you will want them?"

The worst thing about this conversation is that I can see how much it means to her. Her eyes are literally pleading with me to tell her that yes, someday I will want kids. And my feelings for my wife are such that I want to reassure her; I want to—*always*—give her anything that will make her happy.

And really, I have nothing against kids. I had a happy childhood. It's not that I *don't* want kids. I just want to be in a position to give my hypothetical kids the same amount of attention, love, and security that my parents gave me, and my lifestyle, such that it is, doesn't afford that luxury right now.

Sure, it's changed, financially-speaking, since marrying Courtney, but not enough to feel that starting a family anytime soon is a responsible choice. Not to mention, I'm still getting used to being married. We're coming up on the two-month mark, not the two-*year* mark. I need time.

I mean, can you imagine a time when you will want them?

"Do we have to talk about this now?"

"Do you hate children?" she counters.

"Of course I don't *hate* children." But, man, I hate this conversation.

"Then what?" she asks, her voice ratcheting up to the next level. "Why can't you even see them as an *eventuality*?"

"Jesus, Court. We're still learning how to handle conflict, how to communicate. We don't have any savings yet. Our incomes are vastly different. I have some career goals I need to work on. I'd like to get a show up and running, or—*God help me*—produced on Broadway. I'd like to travel with you and see some more of the world. And these are things that need to happen without a kid in the mix."

Her face is stony. "You still haven't answered my question."

"*What?* Can I see kids as an eventuality?"

"Yes!" she says. "Can you see it or not, Josh?"

Staring at this woman, whom I love, to whom I am promised for the rest of my life, I search my heart for an answer—for the *real* answer—to her question.

And it shocks me, but suddenly my heart stops pounding.

I stare at the blue of her eyes and the curve of her cheek.

I take in the blonde wisps of hair near her temples that have already started to dry in the sun.

I drop my gaze to the full pinkness of her lips.

And suddenly...out of nowhere...my mind offers up the image of a blond-haired, blue-eyed cherub who looks exactly like her mother. She's running toward me in the sunshine—with the same take-me-to-my-knees smile as her mother, little arms outstretched and blue eyes trusting me, down to the smallest particle of her soul.

In that moment, in a sparkling blue pool with my wife demanding answers I'm barely able to give, I get it.

I can see how loving someone like I love Courtney could make me consider—even, on some nebulous level, *want*—to make a baby and start a family with her. I can see myself loving that child with a same, but different, intensity that I love my wife.

And I find it's not as terrifying or daunting a thought as it's been in the past.

One child, I think.

One quiet, well-mannered, sweet-smelling, child.

We could pack her up and take her with us on trips, and besides, one kid wouldn't cost *that* much, right? If we saved up for a few years, got our finances in shape, and moved a little further down the road in our careers? Yeah. Maybe it could work out. Maybe it could even be good.

It surprises the hell out of me to admit it to myself, but yes, I *can* see it...in the far, far*, far, very distant* future, I think I can see being a father.

"Yeah," I say, looking deeply into her eyes and realizing a love for her so deep, I cannot begin to fathom where it started or how it could ever end. "*With you*...I can see it."

She gasps, covering her mouth with her hands as tears brighten her eyes. Oh, fuck.

"But...*not*...*now*," I say firmly, putting my hands on her shoulders. "And...and only *one* kid."

"One would be great! One would be...*everything*! You mean it?" she asks breathlessly.

"Someday. Maybe. Yeah."

"A year?" she asks. "Two?"

My eyes widen and I give her a look that says she's really pushing it now.

Courtney pretends to zip her mouth closed and throws the key over her shoulder, but she can't keep her smile to herself. It widens and widens until she throws her arms around my neck and leans up on tiptoes to kiss me.

"I love you so much," she says, then kisses me again.

Through the nylon of her bathing suit, I feel her nipples harden into tight points, and she arches her back, which makes blood course to my cock, flooding it, hardening it.

"Let's go upstairs," she suggests in a husky voice.

She takes my hand and heads for the pool stairs, and I am only too happy to follow her. This is interesting. Even *talking* about a potential baby someday has this effect on my wife, huh? Another plus to throw into the equation, I guess.

We run up the back stairs like a couple of kids, bursting into our bedroom and barely closing the door before we're pulling at each other's suits as we passionately kiss. Because I can't wait to get inside of her, I turn us around so that her back is against the wall, lift her just enough to get my cock situated, then slide her back down until I'm fully sheathed.

"Ahhh, Court...fuck, you feel good."

"Love me, Josh," she murmurs, her hands locked at the base of my neck, her lips sucking and teeth biting my ear lobe.

It hurts, but it also heightens my excitement and I'm throbbing inside of her with every thrust. She's deliciously hot and wet, and our bodies are still slick from the pool, and we slide against each other like our skin's been oiled. Faster than usual, she's crying out my name, her pussy walls clenching my cock in rhythmic waves as she lets her head fall back against the wall. I drive up into her twice more, then come in hot streams of cum, again and again, filling her completely and panting with satisfaction against her neck.

Somehow, I maneuver us to the bed, where we fall on top of the comforter in a heap, still intimately joined together.

"I love you," she sighs, lying beneath me with her eyes closed. "You make me so happy."

I kiss her gently, tenderly, before rolling onto my back beside her. "I love you too."

I stare up at the ceiling for a moment, surprised when that image of a blonde, blue-eyed baby girl flits softly through my mind.

In fact, it's the last thing I think about as my wife nestles into my side and we both fall asleep.

***

<u>Courtney</u>

For the two weeks following our stay at the Overlook, Josh and I fucked liked rabbits and I'm not kidding. We couldn't keep our hands off of each other.

What he said at the B&B? That he'd be open to having a child with me? It meant everything to me, and I can't stop thinking about it.

In fact, it forced me to make a pretty important decision soon after we returned to the city. While we were away, I realized that the purse holding my birth control pills, which I thought I'd left in the car, had actually been left at home. I didn't say anything to Josh, because I didn't want to freak him out, but when we returned to the city on Sunday night, I went out for an evening run and stopped in at Duane Reade for a morning-after pill, Plan B. As Josh slept soundly in our bed that night, I sat on the toilet in our bathroom, staring at the pill that would prevent any possible pregnancy from taking root.

I won't lie; I considered not taking it. I imagined myself saying—three or four months from now when I "discovered" I was pregnant—*"I left my purse in the city that weekend. I didn't realize!"*

But the more I considered deceiving him, the guiltier I felt.

Josh had agreed to hear "my truth," and to discuss it, whatever it was. And—*against all odds*—he'd found room in his heart to not only consider having a baby, but to even agree that he'd be open to having "one kid" at some point in the future.

How could I, in turn, betray that trust, tricking him into a pregnancy he wasn't ready for quite yet?

It had hurt to take that bitter pill, washing it down with a glass of water and a few tears, but I did it. I did it because what Josh and I are creating in our marriage is precious to me. I love and respect him too much to trap him into a situation when he's already asked for a little more time.

Besides, the next day at work, my schedule got especially busy. In a move that genuinely surprised me, Joel Morris put me officially in charge of the Scandinavian project.

While I was relieved—trusting me with the project indicated a certain amount of job security that I really need right now—the fact that managing this deal also includes a lot of European travel away from Josh sucks. Since our brief getaway to the Overlook two weeks ago, I've spent four days in Stockholm, and today I arrive in Copenhagen for more meetings.

As I check in at the Herman K Hotel, I look up to find a collection of clocks behind the front desk. It's three o'clock in the afternoon here, and ten o'clock at night in New York. My mind immediately thinks about Josh. Since it's a Friday, he's not working. I wonder if he's out with friends or home.

God, I wish he was here.

It clutches my heart like a rubber band, this almost-strangling longing for my husband. It steals my breath and makes my eyes burn with tears. If I still had my trust fund, I'd link up to the hotel wi-fi, buy Josh a first-class ticket, and fly him here for the weekend. Alas, I think such a gesture would only upset him since we're supposed to be saving.

"We have you checking in for three nights, Ms. Dalton?"

"Yes."

"You have a balcony-double reserved."

"Great," I mutter.

"Can we send up anything for you?"

"No, *tak*," I answer, mustering a small smile.

I'll order room service later, after I've had a chance to call Josh and go over the numbers for tomorrow's meeting.

The hotel clerk swipes my credit card and gives me a small wallet with my room keycard, wishing me a pleasant stay and telling me to call down to the front desk if I need anything.

It's a beautifully-designed hotel, industrial-chic and very Scandinavian, but it feels impossible to enjoy it alone. If I was with my husband, we'd be noticing every detail together, pointing out interesting art and exclaiming over the funky light fixtures. By myself, I just long for the comfort of my room so I can text Josh and feel his presence for a while.

Three more days. It feels like forever.

And that's when it occurs to me that this is the first time I've ever been in love and away from the person I love. I remember a passage from one of my favorite books, Jane Eyre: Mr. Rochester is speaking of his affection for Jane and says, *"i sometimes have a queer feeling with regard to you—especially when you are near me, as now: it is as if i had a string somewhere under my left ribs, tightly and inextricably knotted to a similar string situated in the corresponding quarter of your little frame. And if that boisterous channel, and two hundred miles or so of land come broad between us, I am afraid that cord of communion will be snapt; and then I've a nervous notion I should take to bleeding inwardly."*

As I stand in the elevator, I find this quote on Goodreads and read it over and over again. I can feel that cord between me and Josh. Right this second, I can feel it. I feel the tension of it as an entire ocean separates us, and I learn something vital about who I am: I am someone who wants to be near her husband. I am someone who doesn't like being apart. And now that I know that, perhaps I can take steps to change it in the future. When I start and run my own firm, it will not be international. Or if it is, I will hire someone else to do the traveling, and I will stay close to home, close to Josh, so that I don't have to feel like this over and over again.

My room is minimalist in decoration but has that luxury-hotel smell of flowers and soap, which I love. I sigh, rolling my suitcase to the foot of the bed and tossing my briefcase on top of the bureau. I toe off my shoes and pull my phone from my jacket pocket, lying back on the huge, lonely bed, and opening a text chat to my husband.

Finally here in Copenhagen. I miss you. I miss you so much it hurts. Only three more nights.

I stare at the screen, willing those three little dots to appear, telling me that he's received my message and is writing back, but they don't. After a few minutes, I place the phone on the bedside table and sit up. Crossing the room, I step out onto my balcony, taking a deep, bracing breath of Danish air when I hear my phone chime. And like that chime determines my living and dying, I race across the room to grab my phone.

I miss you too.

Heading back to the balcony, I stop at the mini bar and grab a small bottle of white wine, unscrewing the top and drinking directly from the bottle as I sit down in a small metal chair outside. By the time I'm seated, another message has appeared:

I have something to tell you.

I type back: *Have you heard back from Simi Frederick already?*

No, he answers. *I only sent in the play a few days ago.*

I know. But it's completely awesome. They should cancel the competition and just hand you first prize.

Not that you're biased, he writes back, adding a smiley-face, heart-eyes emoji.

I am biased, of course, but I was also blown away by *Miss Gibbs Will See You Now*. When I finished reading, I looked up at Josh, who had been watching me, and I said, "Remember when we saw Sam's play? And you asked me if it was a winner?"

He'd nodded. "Yeah. You said it was good, but not a winner."

"*Thi*s," I'd said, holding up the bound script, "is a winner, Josh. *This* is amazing."

Not unlike the guy who wrote *Memoirs of a Geisha*, my

husband had somehow managed to tap into the brain of a woman from the 1890s, making her struggle to find her independence real and relatable. I cried. I laughed. I wished the ghost of Kate Chopin could rise and judge the competition herself. And if Josh doesn't win first prize and see his play staged, I will do anything I have to, to personally make his play a reality. It's that good. And I believe in him and his future as a playwright more than ever.

LET IT BE KNOWN, I type. *My husband is the most talented playwright that ever was.*

Ever? he asks.

Okay. Since Shakespeare.

He sends a red heart emoji, and I take another sip of wine. *Hey! What do you need to tell me? Is Sam hitting on you again?*

Those three dots appear and stay on my screen for a long time, cycling for a while and piquing my curiosity. Finally, a long message appears, and I need to scroll up to find the beginning.

Your dad called me this afternoon. I have no idea how he got my number, but he called to ask if I'd be willing to have a drink with him. I was tempted to refuse, but his invitation was respectful, so I agreed to meet him. We went to Merchant's, and I expected him to be difficult, but he wasn't, Court. He was sorry. He said he was sorry for suggesting we divorce. He said he would reinstate your trust and asked that we spend Labor Day weekend out in Connecticut. I told him you were in Denmark until next week, and he asked if we'd come out for your birthday weekend instead.

I bite my upper lip. *What did you say?*

I told him I needed to talk to you, and that I'd let him know.

But, babe, I think we should go.

I take a deep breath and another sip of wine. I can't help but wondering if my father is trying to manipulate me here. A few weeks ago, he cut me off. Now he wants to reinstate my trust and have us come and visit? What's the catch?

I don't know if I trust him.

I have to tell you something else, writes Josh.

What?

The three dots appear again, then disappear, then appear again. *Want me to call you?*

You're making me nervous. Just write it.

Your mom's sick, Court.

What are you talking about?

She has cancer, he writes. *Stage II Melanoma.*

I press Josh's number and the call goes through immediately.

"Court?"

"What are you talking about?" I repeat, my heart beating so fast that I press my free hand to my chest.

"Your mom was diagnosed with Stage Two Melanoma. She's been getting treatment at Sloan Kettering."

"Jesus!" I race to my briefcase, open it, and pull out my laptop, signing into the hotel's wi-fi as I cradle the phone between my shoulder and ear. "When did this happen?"

"Recently. Your dad said that she had the surgery last week—"

"What *surgery*?" I demand in a shriek.

"They removed two tumors from her left shoulder," he

says. "They recommended chemo just to be sure any remaining cancer cells are gone."

When the wi-fi connects, I type "melanoma stage 2 prognosis" into the Google search engine and press enter.

"Court? Baby, you there?"

"Yeah," I say, clicking on a link to find out how much longer my mother has to live.

"Listen, he said that the surgery went great. They had to cut deep, but they're pretty sure they got it all. They're doing a biopsy now, and they'll know more next week."

"Uh-huh," I murmur, scanning the screen.

It appears that the prognosis for five-year survival is 70-81%, depending on whether it was Stage 2A or Stage 2B.

"A or B?" I ask him.

"What?"

"Stage 2A or Stage 2B? My mom's cancer."

"I don't—I don't know. I think A."

"Eighty-one percent," I whisper.

"What?"

"She has an eighty-one percent chance of living five more years," I say.

"Yeah," says Josh. "Your dad says she's doing really well too."

"I should call her, right? I should call my mom. Right now. I need to—"

"You should definitely call her," Josh says, "but you should calm down a little first."

"I'm calm."

"No, babe. You're in shock and you're upset," he says.

"Don't call her like that, okay? Talk to me for a little bit. Calm down a little."

I didn't realize it before now, but my cheeks are covered with tears. When did I start crying?

"I'm—I'm crying," I say.

"I know," he says. "I could hear it in your voice. Breathe deep, babe. Breathe. It's okay."

"M-My mom has c-cancer," I choke out as the floodgates open.

"But she's okay," says Josh, his voice low and soothing. "Listen to me; she's okay. They cut out the tumors. She's getting chemo. She's doing good, babe. I promise. Your dad said she's doing okay." I'm still crying so he keeps talking. "Your father said that your mother getting sick was like a wake-up call for them. They don't want to be on bad terms with you...with us. They want peace."

Sniffling, I manage to say, "I—I w-want that t-too."

"Shhhh. It's scary, but she's okay," hums Josh. "Hey, what are you doing now?"

"S-Standing over m-my...laptop," I say.

"Lie down in bed," he says. "I'll go into the bedroom and lie down too."

I do as he says, though I still protest, "I should c-call my m-mom."

"It's after ten o'clock and I'm sure she's sleeping," he says. "You can call her in the morning, okay? Are you lying down?"

I sniffle. "Y-Yeah."

"You lie on your right side and I'll lie on my left so

we're facing each other, okay?"

"Okay."

"Close your eyes and just listen to my voice…"

And this, I realize, as he speaks to me softly of reconciliations and mended fences, is one of the deeper and more intimate moments of my entire marriage so far. In the only way he can, he stays with me, he comforts me, he loves me through this crisis. Though an ocean separates us, and that thread beneath my heart is taut with longing, I know that he loves me. I know that he supports me. I feel certain that as long as we hold onto each other, despite any distance between us, our growing love can see us through any storm.

That's what I hope.

That's what I think.

And in some sure corner of my naïve and foolish heart, that's what I'm sure is so.

CHAPTER 8
• CELEBRATIONS •

"When it comes to holidays and traditions, borrow some from your childhood to share with your spouse, but also consider creating new and different traditions, unique to the new family you're building together."
--Dr. Sydney Morningstar

<u>Josh</u>

By the start of fall, after a summer of growing together and adjusting to being newlyweds, Courtney and I have officially settled into "married life." It feels like we're coasting now—like we've found our rhythm, and it is bliss.

During the week, she leaves for work in the morning, and I'm at Tidewaters by the time she comes home from the office. Some days I go to the New Dramatists to work on one of my plays, and other days I do the grocery shopping or fix little things around the apartment, like the leaky faucet in the kitchen or the deadbolt on the front door that keeps getting stuck. When I come home from bartending, I shower before indulging in my favorite part of every day: sliding naked into bed beside my wife.

I think we both live for weekends...for the uninterrupted time we spend together. Sometimes we meet up with friends—hers or mine—at a bar or for dinner, but to be honest, our favorite weekends are the ones we spend exclusively together, reading our books on the rooftop terrace, sharing long coffee dates at a nearby café, getting cheap, last-minute TKTS tickets to a show we haven't seen, or just lounging in bed for hours, telling secrets and laughing and loving each other in new and different ways.

We are both besotted. Completely.

Courtney's mother has already undergone two rounds of chemotherapy, and Court was with her for both, stopping by during her lunchbreak to sit with her mom while she received targeted therapy to her shoulder. Her prognosis is very good, since the tumors weren't ulcerated, and both mother and daughter feel positive about the future, for which I am grateful.

Reuniting with Courtney's parents and having her trust reinstated has been a mixed blessing. On one hand, I liked the progress we were making as a couple, saving our money and focused on joint financial responsibility for our future. But on the other hand, having quasi-unlimited funds means that we can change up our lives whenever we choose to.

"Hey," she says as I plate dinner for us on a Friday night, "I want to ask you something."

I place sour cream on the table for our baked potatoes and take a seat across from her. "What's up?"

She cuts into her steak and hums with satisfaction as she chews. "You're a really good cook, you know that?"

"Mom insisted," I say, grinning at her.

I try to plan something nice for Friday evening, and steak is my girl's favorite thing for dinner.

"So...you know how I've got my trust back," she says.

"Yep."

"And you know how much I hate working with Joel."

"Mm-hm."

"What if I quit?" she blurts out.

I blink at her mid-bite. "What do you mean?"

"What if I quit DeWitt, Morris & Jones and start my own firm?"

I place my fork on the side of my plate and take a gulp of beer. "I thought you said it was important to make partner before you left."

"It would be *ideal* to make partner," she says, "but if I finish this deal on a high note, it might be better to leave now...you know, before things go south with Joel again."

"So...you're thinking about quitting when?"

"Probably just after the first of the year."

"Wow. That's soon."

"This deal will be done by Thanksgiving. I'd quit in December, but I want my bonus."

"What about insurance?" I ask.

"The trust. We'll pay for it out of pocket."

"How much does it cost to set up your own company? Do you have any potential clients? Potential deals to start working on?"

"Umm...I don't know...not yet...and not yet," she says, "but I had lunch with Dina today, and I asked if she'd consider coming to work for me. She said she would."

"Would you need to rent an office? What would that cost?"

"I don't know," she says, picking up her wineglass and leaning away from the table.

"Or would you want to work from the guest room?"

"Honestly, babe, I don't know yet."

I stare at her because I really don't want to be unsupportive of her dreams, but I'm concerned she's being impulsive because she doesn't like her boss. Frankly, it doesn't sound like she's given this much thought.

"I'll have to come up with a plan," she says quickly. "I just wanted to know what you thought of quitting as a concept."

"As a concept? Yeah, sure. I love it. I think it sucks that you have to work for someone whom you don't like or respect. But there have got to be fifty steps between where you are right now and owning and operating a successful business. You can't just skip them."

She sighs loudly, taking a sip of wine and giving me a look over the rim of the glass.

"What?"

"*Fifty* steps? I think you're being overdramatic," she says. "Here's an example in *your* world...if you win Simi's competition and someone catches your play and loves it, you could run off-Broadway for a while before getting a possible Broadway run." She counts off on her fingers. "Competition. Lincoln Center. Off-Broadway. Broadway. By my count, that's four steps to make your dream come true, not fifty."

My mouth drops open. "Do you really think it's *that* easy?"

"Yeah. I guess I do."

"Do you know how much work will need to go into directing and producing my show if I even *win* that competition?"

"A lot."

"Yeah, babe. *A lot*. I'll have to quit bartending at Tidewaters. The rest of my plays will be totally ignored for the next few months and I could lose my seat at the New Dramatists. I don't know how much we'll even see each other. I'll practically be *living* at Lincoln Center from October through February."

"I get it. I'm all for it. Doing great things takes a lot of hard work."

"Which is why quitting your job before you look into how to set up shop as a new firm worries me."

She takes a deep breath and holds it before letting it go, an injured expression taking over her face. "How come—when it's *your* big dream—I'm one hundred percent ready to support you, but when it's *my* big dream, you throw up roadblocks?"

"Come on," I say. "That's not fair. I was asking reasonable questions and you had no answers for any of them."

"I can figure out the answers," she says, picking up her barely-eaten dinner plate and carrying it into the kitchen.

"Of course you can! All I'm saying is maybe figure them out *before* you quit. That's all."

She's standing at the kitchen sink when I realize she's crying. *Crying*. Over *this*? We were just talking, weren't we?

I get up from the table and stand behind her, spinning

her gently by the shoulders and pulling her into my arms. I'm grateful when she doesn't fight me. She just steps forward, resting her head on my shoulder as she cries.

"I r-ruined dinner," she says.

"Nah."

"You m-made steaks and p-potatoes and—"

"It's okay," I whisper.

"I don't know why I'm so—so s-sensitive tonight."

"Long week?" I ask. "Jerky boss?"

She sniffles and nods against me. "Yeah. Every meeting I have with Joel is awful. He's argumentative and patronizing. I *know* I'm doing a good job, but I'm not getting the credit I deserve."

"Can others see how hard you're working?" Her tears are subsiding now, and she leans back a little to look up at me. "I think so. Mr. DeWitt passed me in the hall today and told me to keep up the good work."

I reach for her face, cupping her cheeks tenderly. "Baby, I don't want you to have to go work somewhere you hate every day. I don't want you to have to work with Joel Morris if you don't want to. He sounds like a first-rate asshole and I'm still totally willing to kick his ass around lower Manhattan if you give me the okay."

She half-sobs, half-giggles. "He'd pee his pants when he saw you coming... but the answer's still no."

I tuck a strand of blonde hair behind her ear. "You want to leave your job? Definitely leave. I'm behind you a hundred and fifty percent. I'll even renovate the guest room into an awesome office for my brilliant wife. All I'm saying is that I think you should have a plan first. Look into what it'll take to set up your own business and make sure that's what you want to do. Then, finish the project you're working on, grab your bonus, give your notice, and get out of there."

"So, you're okay with it?"

"Theoretically, yeah. As long as you've got a solid plan." She sniffles again, and more tears follow. I hold her closer. "Hey…are you okay? You seem…*really* emotional."

"I—I don't know what's wrong with me," she says. "I'm probably coming down with something. I've been tired and emo all week."

"Maybe get into bed early?" I suggest. "You've been working really hard lately, Court."

"Y-Yeah," she says. "Sleep sounds good."

"How about I bring you some mint tea in bed?"

"You are so the best," she says, wiping her eyes as she steps out of my arms. She gives me a quick kiss on the cheek before she heads back to the bedroom.

I stand against the counter as she goes, flicking a glance at her uneaten meal in the sink, and recognizing a slightly uneasy feeling in the pit of my stomach that I can't totally explain.

***

October 1st dawns on a Tuesday, and I'm awake before Courtney, staring at the bedside clock which reads 5:45am.

At some point today, after 10:00am ET, the winners of the Boston Emerging Playwright competition will be notified by Simi Frederick, and I am hoping—with every cell in my body—that my name is first on the winners' list. This is one competition where coming in any place but first would suck. Second and third place winners receive a check, but only the first-place winner receives enough money to properly produce the winning play and a weeklong run on the Mitzi Newhouse stage at Lincoln Center.

If I win, I'll be able to cast the play, costume and set it, hire decent lighting and sound guys, and—if I choose—direct it. I'll have world-class stage managers on loan from Lincoln Center, a professionally-printed Playbill, and mentions in top Broadway magazines. It's one of the biggest and best playwriting competitions in the country, and I can barely contain my mixture of nerves and excitement.

Getting up quietly so that I don't wake up Courtney, I throw on boxers, sweat shorts, and a T-shirt, then slip out of our bedroom. I'll take an early morning run to get rid of my nerves and pick up two iced coffees at Starbucks. Court loves her Starbucks.

On my run, I think about last weekend.

When I brought Courtney her tea in bed on Friday night, she was already asleep. We hit the Met on Saturday, but when I suggested drinks with Max and Mia on Saturday night, she said she was tired and asked if we could stay in. I think she must have been fighting off a little bug because she slept hard on Saturday and Sunday nights too.

Yesterday, I barely saw her, but she didn't wake up when I got home from work, even though I was hard as a rock and ready to play, per usual.

Part of me wonders if something else is going on with her—if maybe she's feeling depressed about work or concerned about her mom. But her mood was pretty chipper for the rest of the weekend, actually. She's probably got a cold like she guessed on Friday night, or maybe she's just a little run-down, I think, shaking off my mild worries and turning my mind back to the competition.

I wasn't kidding when I told Courtney that winning the contest would mean big changes in our lives. I will need to quit my job at Tidewaters, because I doubt Lulu would let me take a four-month leave of absence. And God, I hope I never need that job again. I know it's a longshot—that my play will win the competition, and that once it does, it will be picked up for a long-term run at a big New York theater, but I can't help hoping. That's the whole point of this entire exercise, isn't it? To finally be discovered.

It's almost seven by the time I head back to our apartment with two iced coffees in hand. I throw my keys on the table in the foyer and head back to the bedroom where I find Courtney sitting up in bed.

And the first thing I notice is that while her eyes are wide, the rest of her face is almost *expressionless*. Like she's hiding a secret.

"Hey!" I say. "Good morning!"

"Good morning," she says, her tone soft and a little stilted.

I scan her eyes, but they give away nothing. "Everything okay?"

"I have something important to tell you."

My eyes flick to the clock, which reads 7:09am. There's no way the winners have been announced yet, so this has to be something else. Now, here's the weird thing—I don't know what I'm expecting her to say, and maybe it's because of the weird expression on her face, but a bolt of panic shoots through me.

"Important good? Or important bad?" I ask, standing beside the bed and offering her the plastic cup of coffee.

She takes it from me and places it on the bedside table. "Give me the other one too."

"Why?" I ask, handing it over.

"Because I think you're about to freak out."

"Why? Are you okay? Is everything okay?" I sit down beside her, the blood draining from my face as I consider the fact that she's been so tired lately. "Are you...sick? You've been so tired. Baby, are you—"

"What? No!" she says, as a huge smile blooms across her face. "No! I'm fine! Josh...YOU WON! Simi Frederick just called. You *won* the competition!"

"What? They're not announcing the...the—"

"—winner until ten? Perks of being family friends!" she exclaims, shucking off the covers and rising to her knees. "She called my mom first because she was so excited, she had to share it with someone, and my mom gave her my cell number and told her to call me. So, she did! You won, Josh! *Miss Gibbs Will See You Now* won!"

"I won?" I jump up, running my hands through my hair, then clasping them on top of my sweaty head. "Babe, are you serious? I won?!"

She nods, clasping her hands together, her eyes tearing as she giggles with glee. "You did! First place! Your play's going to Lincoln Center!"

"Court! Do you know what this means? I won!" I cry, putting my hands under her arms and pulling her up so I can kiss her. "I love you! I won! I'm going to Lincoln Center!"

She's laughing and crying, and I'm laughing and crying, holding onto her so hard, because I can't believe it, and yet it's happening, right here, right now, right this second.

All of my dreams are coming true.

***

Courtney

When Josh said he wouldn't be around much if his play won, he wasn't kidding.

Not that I thought he was.

I just didn't realize exactly how little I would see him.

We went from spending our weekends exclusively with each other to him spending long hours at the theater, casting his show, working with scene and costumer designers, and getting everything ready for rehearsals to start in December.

And me?

Well, by mid-October, I had to face the truth about something I was trying hard to ignore.

When I didn't get my period on September 15th, I didn't freak out. I logged onto the internet and read the facts about Plan B, doing all sorts of arithmetic in my mind. We had unprotected sex on Saturday afternoon, and I took the pill on Sunday night…about 30 hours later. And I don't know why I thought Plan B was 100% foolproof, but taken between 24-72 hours after sex, it's only 89% effective. Then again, I also read something that calmed me: ...*it is possible that levonorgestrel may cause your next period to be heavier or lighter than usual. It may also come earlier or later than is normal for you.* So, okay, I thought. My period's just coming a bit later than usual because of Plan B messing up my cycle. No worries.

But today is October 15th, and my period hasn't come since August. And I can't deny the fact that for two or three weeks now, I've been more tired than usual, although I can't say I've had any other side effects that might indicate a pregnancy. No breast tenderness. No nausea or vomiting. Plus, my mom's been sick, and I just got married—maybe the stress of so many life changes has finally caught up with me? That's possible, right?

Knowing that Josh will be at the theater until late tonight, I swing by Duane Reade on my way home and buy a test by Clear Blue Easy.

The little bag crinkles by my side as I walk home, and my feelings are all over the place. On one hand, I want a child more than almost anything. On the other, we've only been married for a few months, we're still getting to know each other, Josh is not on board with having a baby yet.

What if I'm pregnant and he rejects the baby? Or asks me to get an abortion?

I step onto the elevator, pressing my free palm to my flat stomach. I couldn't do that. I couldn't kill my baby. *Our* baby.

What if he says it's the baby or him?

My heart twists. I love him. I love him so much. I was willing to give up my family and trust fund to have him in my life. But am I willing to give up our child?

I feel like if I did that…if I aborted a baby I want, that I would end up hating him. That the regret would be so bitter, it would eat up all the sweetness between us, and not only would the baby be gone, but our marriage would die anyway.

My hands are shaking when I sit down on the toilet and take the pregnancy test out of its foil package. Leaning forward just a touch, I pee on the stick, then cover it with a blue plastic top, and place it on the vanity counter beside me. I set the stopwatch on my phone. In five minutes, I'll know.

"What do you want it to say?" I whisper, wiping myself and flushing the toilet, careful to avoid looking at the little window on the test when I stand up and take a seat on the rim of the tub to wait.

Josh has been clear with me from the beginning of our marriage: he's not ready for kids. Even in August when he said he'd be "open" to "one kid," he wasn't enthusiastic. I think, ideally, Josh wants two or three years to be ready. He definitely doesn't want this. Not right now. My knees bounce with nervous energy, my heels occasionally clacking against the tile floor as I wait for my phone to ding.

I think about that night six months ago, when I was sitting on a barstool at Tidewaters and told him I wanted to get married. His face was so shocked, like he couldn't believe what I was saying. My mind slides forward to our wedding day—to seeing him standing there by the altar in Scotland, waiting for me. And then I fast forward again to our party when his dreadful ex was questioning our reasons for marrying each other, and he told her that he was in love with me.

We've come so far in such a short amount of time. From friends to spouses to lovers to partners.

Are we ready to add "parents" too?

My heart sinks, because as much as I'd like to believe we're ready, we're not. He's not. The timing is terrible.

Josh is spending every waking moment at Lincoln Center staging his play and I am trying to finish my deal at work, after which I'll need to put time and energy into starting my own business. If I *am* pregnant—I do some quick calculations—I'm about ten weeks along, I guess. Two and a half months. And a pregnancy lasts nine months, right? So...our baby would come sometime in May. Could I get a business up and running by then? Unlikely. Which means I'm trapped at DeWitt, Morris & Jones? No way. I'm *not* staying there a day longer than I have to. I guess I could just—

My phone dings, telling me that the longest five minutes of my life has come and gone, and I take a deep breath and hold it as I stand up and take a tentative step toward the sink.

Pregnant.

I blink at the test, picking it up with shaking fingers.

Pregnant.

No "Not" preceding it, even though I twist my wrist, changing the angle of the stick in the light to make sure.

Carefully, like it's made of precious glass, I place the stick back down on the vanity, hugging myself as I leave the bathroom. I'm pregnant. Oh my God. I'm about ten weeks pregnant.

Tears course down my cheeks as I sit down on the edge of the bed and cover my stomach with one palm over the other.

I need to go out to Greenwich to see my OB/GYN.

I need to stop drinking wine.

I need to find out what things I'm not supposed to be eating.

Oh my God. We'll need to turn the guest bedroom into a nursery! Or maybe start thinking about buying that house out in the country? I need to find out if it's a boy or a girl. I need—

I need to tell Josh.

My heart plummets.

I race back to the bathroom and grab my phone, typing "when does a pregnancy start showing?" into my search bar. After a moment, several articles pop up, and I scan them, desperate to find an answer that will give me a little more time.

Most new mothers will begin to show at 14-16 weeks.

"New mothers," I sob, feeling so happy and so sad at the same time. A mother. I'm going to be a mother and I'm already so in love with the idea, I know that there's nothing in the world—not even my husband's reticence—that could induce me to get rid of my baby. I'm keeping it. And hopefully—*Oh, God, please*—Josh will be able to accept it, to love it as much as I already do.

I have four to six weeks before he'll notice, and I'm not stick thin, so probably closer to six. Six weeks. The end of November. By the end of November, I *have* to tell him.

Right after Thanksgiving, I think, reminding myself to wrap the test in tissue and throw it down the incinerator before he comes home. *I'll give him a little more time to get his play humming along and then I'll tell him.*

"Until then, little one," I whisper to my baby, cupping my

belly tenderly, "it's just you and me."

***

Five weeks later, Josh and I are on a plane to Minneapolis, and it blows my mind that I've been able to keep the secret for this long.

Honestly, his rigorous schedule at the theater is the only thing that's made it possible.

He doesn't notice little details right now—like if I'm drinking tea instead of wine, or that my breasts have increased by a size. Okay. He might have noticed that, but I told him I was eating a lot of fast food at work while I close my deal, and I needed to go on a diet when it was finished. He'd looked at my bigger breasts with hungry eyes and told me not to dare.

I've seen my OB/GYN out in Greenwich twice, which was easy to explain away by visiting my parents while he was working. My calculations were right, and Baby Dalton should be arriving right around May 20th. Everything looks normal and perfect, and aside from avoiding alcohol, sushi, and raw cheese, my doctor said to live my life as usual.

Luckily, I've also had a really easy first trimester. No nausea or vomiting, and my days of marked fatigue are already behind me as I enter my second trimester.

But living with this secret has also been exhausting. I need to tell my husband. The thing is, as the days go by, and I feel great, I come up with myriad excuses not to tell him…yet.

The costumes came in and he loves them…*don't tell him today.*

The actress he was hoping would audition for Pippa showed up…*don't tell him today.*

He needs to write copy for an article on Broadway.com...*don't tell him today.*

He's exhausted from re-designing the lighting...*don't tell him today.*

And now here I am, headed out to Minneapolis to meet his family, and I've reached my deadline. I have to tell him. Either while we're there, or on the ride home, but I have promised myself that I will not set foot again in New York until he knows the truth.

He's going to be a father in approximately six months...whether he loves the idea or not.

The good thing about all of this extra time is that I've been able to prepare myself for any response on his part. For anger. For a panic attack. For a tantrum. For silence. For a possible, but hopefully not long-term, separation.

That's the response that hurts my heart the most: Josh pulling away from me. Josh wanting a separation, or—*please God, no*—Josh wanting a divorce. I've forced myself to come to terms with the words: *This isn't what I signed up for, Court. I can't do it. I want a divorce.* But they make my eyes swim with tears every time. Losing him would be an almost-unsurvivable catastrophe. It would leave my life, and my heart, in shreds. I'd only keep going for the sake of our baby.

And so I've taken up praying...I've even stopped by Josh's little Lutheran church a couple of times, though he's too busy to join me right now. I sit in the old, wooden pews and I pray that God will intercede; that He will open Josh's heart to love his child, and to keep loving me.

"Ladies and gentlemen, we're about to begin our descent

to the Minneapolis-St. Paul International Airport. Please return your tray tables to the upright and locked position, stow any carry-on luggage, and put your seat in a full and upright position. We should be on the ground in about twelve minutes."

Josh has been making notes to the script, but he tucks it into his backpack and locks his tray table up. Turning to me, he takes my hand, lacing his fingers through mine.

"You good? No turbulence this time."

"I know," I say. "Smooth flight."

"I think I got the cable car scene perfect now. You know the one? When Pippa tells her husband about the book?"

"Mm-hm."

"Hey," he says, tilting his handsome face to the side. "Are you nervous?"

Meeting his parents pales in comparison to telling him my secret at some point over the next five days. "No. I've had so many conversations with your mom at this point, I really feel like I know her."

"She's so excited to finally meet you in person."

"Me too."

"Family's everything to her."

"I know," I say.

Josh sighs. "She's probably going to ask us about having kids."

My skin prickles. "And what will you say?"

"That it's not the right time for us."

I swallow over the lump in my throat. "When will be the right time, again?"

"Maybe in a few years. When you've quit your job and started up your new company. When *Miss Gibbs Will See You Now* wins its first Tony." He grins at me. "Two or three years. Isn't that sort of what we agreed?"

"Sort of." My heart is pounding. "What if it happened sooner?"

His brow furrows for a second. "What do you mean...*happened*? You're on the pill."

"I know. But..."

"But what? Isn't the pill foolproof?"

"Sure," I say, "if you take it at the same time every day."

"And you do, right?"

"Um...yeah. But I guess...sometimes...mistakes can happen."

"Huh? How? You take the pill every day, we don't get pregnant," he says, turning slightly to look out the window.

I'm so close to telling him, the words are forming in my head, sitting on the tip of my tongue, about to make themselves known.

But we did. Remember that weekend in August? I asked you where my purse was? It wasn't in the room or in the car. It was back at our apartment. And in that purse was my pill-pack, so I missed two in a row. I knew how you felt about having a baby, so I took the morning-after pill when we got home, but it didn't work. I'm pregnant, Josh. I'm fifteen weeks pregnant. It just...happened.

Is this the moment? Could this possibly be the right moment?

Jesus, Courtney, no. You're landing in Minneapolis in ten minutes. No, no, no. Don't do it. Not now.

Don't tell him today.

And yet…

"Josh!" I say, my voice urgent.

"What?" he says, turning his head to look at me. His eyes search mine. His fingers squeeze mine gently. "What's up?"

"We're…we're going to have a great Thanksgiving," I say. *Chickenshit. Chickenshit. Chickenshit.*

His lips turn up in a bright, beautiful smile and he kisses me on the cheek. "Ya betcha."

CHAPTER 9
• COMMUNICATION •

"Breakdowns in communication are inevitable. The solution is to keep trying until you figure out a way to get through to each other. No matter how hard."

--Dr. Sydney Morningstar

<u>Courtney</u>

I have waited until the last possible second.

I promised myself I would tell Josh about my pregnancy before my feet touched down in New York again, and since we're back on the plane headed home, I have less than three hours left.

There were plenty of times in Minnetonka when I could have told him, and once when I almost did.

The morning after Thanksgiving, I woke up with a rash on the insides of my arms. I assumed it was due to the cooler weather making my skin dry, or maybe Joanie using a detergent on the bed sheets that was aggravating to my skin, but it was itching so badly, it woke me up. Josh was still sleeping but I could smell coffee brewing in the kitchen, so I pulled on my robe and slipped downstairs to see if Joanie had an antihistamine.

"Good morning, hon!" she exclaimed, bustling across

the little kitchen to hug me hello.

I leaned against her, breathing in the homey smells of fresh laundry, coffee, and bacon. "I'm making more eggs and bacon. You want some?"

Leaning away from her, I grinned. "I'm starving. I'd love some."

"Sit yourself down, then. I'll getcha some."

Pushing up the sleeve of my robe, I showed Joanie the rash. "Hey…I was just wondering if you had some Benadryl? I've got some kind of a rash starting here and it's—"

When she gasped, I stopped speaking and raised my eyes to her face. She was covering her mouth with one hand, her eyes filling with tears as she shook her head back and forth.

"Joanie?" I said, reaching out a hand to her. "Are you okay?"

"Oh, Courtney!" She lurched forward, cupping my cheeks in her hands, a glorious smile, so much like my husband's, lighting up her face. "When are ya due?"

The blood must have drained from my face, because she guided me to a kitchen chair and sat down across from me.

"You're expecting, right?"

"How did you know?" I whispered.

"That there's prurigo of pregnancy, hon. I had it with all three of mine."

"Pruri…what?"

"Prurigo," she said, taking my arm and laying it flat on the table. Gently, she pushed up the sleeve of my robe and looked at the clusters of small, angry papules. "Oh, my. Look at you."

"Can it hurt the baby?"

"Oh, no," she assured me. "Just a bother for momma."

For...momma. Oh, how my heart swelled to hear the words.

"Joanie," I whispered, taking her hands in mine. "He...he doesn't know yet. I haven't told him. He's so busy with the show, I—I didn't want to upset him. Please don't—"

"Huh. I see. Well, it's not my news to tell, now, is it? Don't you worry," she said, squeezing my hands. "And I've got some cream that'll cool that right off. You wait right here."

We spoke briefly again about my pregnancy on Saturday when Josh and his brothers were playing football on the back lawn.

"Just outta curiosity, hon...why haven't you told him yet?" asked Joanie, coming up beside me on the back porch, where I was watching my husband get trounced.

"He doesn't want kids."

"What?! Of course he—"

"No, he doesn't. Not yet," I said, sighing.

"Honey," she said, looking meaningfully at my belly, hidden under a thick sweater, "this isn't a secret you can keep fer much longer."

"You promised you wouldn't tell him."

"Oh, and I won't—I'd never do that—but I do think, sooner than later...you *should*."

"I will." I waved to Josh as he somehow managed to get the ball. "I promised myself I'd tell him before Thanksgiving weekend was over."

"That only leaves today and tomorrow."

"The plane," I told her. "I'll tell him on the plane. He won't be able to escape. He'll be forced to talk to me about it."

She gave me a small smile. "I'll pray for you both. A child is such a blessing. God's greatest blessing. Joshua will see that. I know it."

We hugged and she called out to her boys, "Lunch is ready! Don't make me wait."

And now, here I am…somewhere between Minneapolis and New York, and it's time. I know it's time.

Josh's emails piled up while we were away visiting his family and he's sitting beside me answering interview questions about his play. I take a deep breath and say, "Can you take a break for a second?"

He doesn't look up. "Uh…I'm slammed, babe. I was hoping to get this done."

"I know," I say, "but I wanted to talk for a few minutes."

"I didn't get to work much at my folks'."

"Um…this won't take too long?"

Why I make this sound like a question is a mystery. I'm nervous. Fuck, I'm so nervous. First, it was just me and the baby. Then, my OB/GYN knew. Now, Joanie knows, and Josh, the reluctant father, still doesn't. He *needs* to know. No matter what the outcome, I have to tell him. Now.

He presses save and closes his laptop. "What's up?"

"Did…" I gulp. Why is this so damn hard?! "Did you have a nice Thanksgiving?"

His eyes slide to his laptop before connecting with mine again. He offers me a small, sheepish smile. "Babe, I *really* need to—"

"I'm pregnant."

It comes out in a whoosh, almost like I've been holding my breath since the evening I saw the word **Pregnant** appear on the Clear Blue Easy test.

His smile vanishes. His lips drop open. He blinks at me. "Josh?" I whisper.

"*What?* What did you just say?"

My cheeks prickle, because his voice is so low, so severe, so…unfamiliar.

"I'm pregnant. I didn't plan it. It just…happened."

He reaches up to rub his chin, then runs his hand through his hair, staring at my face, like he's waiting— *hoping?*—for me to say I'm kidding.

"I'm not kidding," I say. "I'm pregnant."

"*Stop saying that*," he hisses, looking away from me. As he stares out the window, I stare at the back of his head. I want to say something else, but I'm frozen, waiting to see what happens next. Suddenly, he unbuckles his seat belt, shoves his laptop in the seatback pocket, jerks up his tray table, and stands up. "I gotta—I gotta go to the bathroom."

"Oh…Okay…"

"Now, Court."

I tuck my legs in, staring up at him, willing him to make

eye contact with me, but he doesn't. He hustles out of our row without a backward glance and enters the bathroom.

Panic attack. Check.

He's freaking out, I tell myself. *You knew this could happen. You knew this probably* would *happen. Be calm. He'll be back in a minute.*

I'm off by nine, but about ten minutes later, he comes out of the bathroom, the hair around his face wet, like it's been splashed repeatedly with water. He sits down beside me, and I face him, waiting for him to look at me. When he does, his eyes are wide and furious.

"What the *hell* are you talking about?"

"I didn't plan it," I say. "It was an accident."

"An *accident.* Your birth control pill didn't get put into your mouth and swallowed down your throat by accident?"

Anger. Check. You were ready for this too.

"The weekend we went to the Hudson Valley. I left my purse at home, remember? And that's where I had my—"

"That was in August," he snaps.

"Yeah."

"That was over three months ago."

"Yeah," I say. My eyes are burning, but I am determined not to cry. It will only make things worse. *Be strong, Courtney. Keep it together.* It's his turn to fall apart.

"How fucking pregnant are you?" he half-whispers, half-growls.

I gulp. "Almost sixteen weeks."

"Fuck!" he shouts.

I look up as the flight attendant rushes over to our row.

"Is everything okay?"

"Yes," I say at the same time Josh says, "No."

"Yes," I say again, lifting my chin. "We're just…talking."

The flight attendant glances at Josh, then back at me before stepping away.

"You did this on purpose," says Josh. "Telling me on a plane so I can't make a scene."

"I know you're upset—"

"You don't know *anything*," he snaps. "What's the cut-off date for—"

Suggesting I abort. Check. Thank God I was ready for this one.

"Don't say it," I tell him firmly. "That's not happening."

"What if I don't want it?"

I take a deep breath and exhale slowly. "It's not an "it." It's our child."

"The fuck it is. I didn't fucking sign on for this, Courtney."

I clear my throat and say, "I didn't make this baby through osmosis, Josh. It takes two to tango."

"You wanted it. I didn't. You…You fucking tricked me into this."

Accusations about betrayal. Yep. Check.

"No," I say as calmly as I can manage. "That's not true. I realized I'd left my pill pack at home once we got back to New York, so that night I went to Duane Reade and bought the morning-after pill. Plan B. I took it that Sunday night. It just…didn't work."

"Fuck this. You're lying."

"I'm not lying. I can show you the receipt. I'm telling you the truth."

Hunching over in his seat, he rubs his forehead with his palm, and even over the din of the plane engine I can hear his breathing, choppy and shallow.

"Hey," I say, brightening my voice, "I know it's not the timing we talked about, but—"

"I'm trapped," he blurts out in a strangled voice. "I'm fucking trapped."

I search my arsenal for this one…for my husband, whom I love, telling me that I've trapped him, for him yelling and cursing about the baby I've come to love, and I realize that I wasn't ready for this one. I don't know what to say, but my impeccable control is chipped away a bit by this particular reaction.

"No one trapped you," I finally say. "It was an accident."

"If that's true," he says, looking up at me with glazed, bloodshot eyes, "then treat it like one."

A sadness so real and so heartbreaking whooshes through me, and my hands immediately cover my stomach, as though protecting my baby from—of all people in the universe—his or her father.

"Be…careful," I choke out. "You're going to say something you'll regret."

"*Regret*?" he cries, his nostrils flaring and spittle collecting between his lips as he sobs. He pauses for a moment, then says, "All I feel…right this moment…is regret."

My breath catches in my lungs, stagnant and still, as I realize he's not just talking about the weekend we made this baby, or the fact that this baby is coming, but he's talking about me. He's talking about our marriage. He's talking about our life together. He's talking about...everything. He doesn't say it. He doesn't have to. I know. In my heart, I know that he's regretting it all. Every single step he's taken since the day I told him I wanted to be married.

For several long, excruciating minutes, we sit side by side, each in our own hell, and I cannot remember a time I have ever felt so alone, so heartbroken, so indescribably sad.

"When we land," I finally say, "we'll move out to Connecticut."

"*We? We* aren't going anywh—"

"The baby and me," I clarify.

"What about your job?"

"The deal wrapped up last week. I'll give my notice."

"You'll lose your bonus."

"I don't care," I murmur, still covering my belly with my hands, and feeling further and further away from my husband with every mile closer to New York.

Another long lapse of silence falls before Josh says, "We'll talk. At some point."

It's a statement, not a question, so I don't answer. I just stare straight ahead, willing this horrific flight to be over.

"Christ, Courtney! I'm too busy for this shit right now," he says, a sudden burst of anger stealing whatever brief bit of composure he'd found. "Your timing sucks."

"My...*timing*?!" I exclaim, snapping my neck to the side to look at him. "We had sex about ten times that weekend. I took a morning-after pill when we got home, and it didn't work. What was I supposed to do, Josh? What would you have done if you were me?"

He looks at me and I can see the answer in his eyes. But, to his credit, he doesn't say the word. Maybe he knows—somehow, someway—that if he suggests I abort this baby a third time, I will not be able to forgive him.

Instead, he says, "I don't know. I don't fucking know, okay? All I know is that the biggest thing in *my whole life*—the only thing I've been working toward since I arrived in New York—is happening right now."

"Yeah," I say, leveling his eyes with mine and wondering how this loving, caring man can be so selfish, so fucking stupid and insensitive when I share the biggest news of our life with him, "I know how that feels. The biggest thing in *my whole life* is happening right now too."

He stares at me for a second and I can see it: I can see his intense love for me—that beautiful, familiar, beloved tenderness for me—cross his features. It lingers for a moment, giving me hope.

Then he sobs softly, clenching his jaw and hissing, "Fuck! Fuck this, Courtney!"

He shakes his head at me like I'm not the person he thought I was, like I've broken his heart forever, and turns to the window.

We don't speak again for the remainder of the flight and my heart breaks a little more with every second of silence.

When we arrive at Newark Airport, I arrange for an Uber car to pick me up. Then, I grab my bag from the overhead bin, turn my back on my husband, and leave the plane without saying goodbye.

***

<u>Josh</u>

The next few days are a nightmare.

A living nightmare.

I arrive at the theater as early as possible, working on autopilot, barking out commands and instructions, barely able to concentrate on what should have been the first triumph of my professional life.

Courtney, and her news, have stolen all of the joy from me, all of the anticipation.

Instead, I'm left with confusion and betrayal, anger and sadness.

I go over and over our conversation on the plane, trying to understand exactly *what* happened, and *how* it happened, and *why* she can't see that starting a family right now is fucking impossible.

I lie in our big, empty bed, staring at the ceiling, fighting with her *in absentia*—demanding why she didn't tell me sooner, why she got to call all the shots and decide if we have the baby or not. We promised not to keep things from each other, and yet, she sat on this—this huge, life-changing news—for weeks, if not months, before finally telling me.

I feel hot tears roll from the corners of my eyes into my

hair when I remember her face on the plane, how brave she was trying to be when she told me, fighting back tears as I yelled and swore at her, and how devastated she looked when I told her I regretted our life together.

I didn't mean it.

If I could tell her anything right now, it would be this: *I don't regret marrying you. I don't regret a moment I've spent with you. I love you so much it aches. I just…don't want to be a father.* I'm not ready. I'm nowhere near ready.

So that's my cycle of pain since returning from Minnesota: confusion, betrayal, anger, and sadness, in a maddening, never-ending loop.

Salt in the wound is that it's Christmastime in New York City, and it used to be my favorite season. As stores decorate their windows and carols float out the door of every restaurant, my loneliness for my wife feels insurmountable. I had everything. And now, I have nothing.

And the thing is? I don't know what I want. Or I do…but I can't have it. I can never have it again because it's gone forever.

I want my wife back! I scream silently.

I want my life back! I sob in the shower.

I want the life that included me and Courtney, spending perfect, magical weekends together, learning about each other and loving one another to distraction.

There is an almost-unspeakable grief that accompanies what I've lost, what was taken away from me, so brutally, so swiftly, so wholly, without contest or quarter.

And the usurper of that idyllic life?

The villain in this particular story?

He or she is the size of a peanut and we're related.

And whether or not I want him or her in my life, he or she is coming.

There is no escape.

There is no hope.

I am trapped in a reality I didn't want, for which I am not at all prepared.

As strange or wrong as it may sound, those are the terms in which I regard my incipient offspring. As someone who has stolen away *something* I loved (my life), *someone* I loved (my wife), and my anger is white-hot and seems endless.

Thank God for it too, because the second I let down my guard—the second I let my anger cool even by a degree or two—my fear is so paralyzing, so all-encompassing, so vast and terrible, I am grateful when I seek and quickly find my anger once again.

It's easier to be furious than frightened.

And that's exactly where my mother finds me. About a week after Courtney and I hugged and kissed her goodbye at the Minneapolis-St. Paul International Airport airport, my mother makes her first trip to New York City in the entirety of my time here.

At first, I think she's an illusion—*I haven't been sleeping very well*—standing in the back of the theater in her sensible, brown wool, traveling coat, holding a small, brown, leather suitcase. But then I see her face. It isn't the face I think about when she crosses my mind—with sparkling eyes and rosy cheeks. Her face is frozen in anger. And shame.

I am in the middle of approving tweaks to the scenery, but it's after five o'clock.

I stick my fingers in my mouth and whistle to get everyone's attention. "Uh! Thank you, everyone, for a great day! Let's, uh, take the weekend off? See you all back here at nine o'clock am on Monday!"

There's an excited buzz throughout the crew to have a couple of days off from our grueling schedule. As they whoop and high-five, I collect my belongings and head up the aisle to my mother.

"Joshua," she says, her blue eyes searing.

"Mom," I say, leaning forward to kiss her cheek. She remains frozen, neither embracing me, nor leaning forward to kiss me back. As I draw away, I say, "I didn't know you were coming."

To put this into perspective: she didn't come to my college graduation or to any of the smaller shows I've self-produced on community stages. No. She waits to come now. Part of me wants to be petulant about this fact, but her expression makes self-pity impossible. She played this well, showing up, by surprise, in person. I could have handled, and maybe even shrugged-off, her intense and unwavering disapproval over the phone. In person? It's impossible.

"I have never been so ashamed of you, Joshua. Never. Not in my entire life."

She says this softly and calmly, without cursing or carrying on, but it's worse than an arsenal of "fuck you"s. There is a midwestern chill in her tone, and it colors her usual voice from warm to icy.

"You don't understand—"

"Here is what I understand: Your wife is pregnant. Your place is beside her. You are *not* beside her. You are not even in the same state as she."

As members of my crew pass us on their way home, they give me curious looks, saying goodnight with raised eyebrows and even a couple of "you're-in-trouble-with-your-mom" grimaces. Furious mothers are a universal dread.

"Can we go somewhere else to talk, please?"

"Oh," she says. "You think I'm here for *you*?"

I stare at her with my mouth open.

"I only *stopped here* en route to Connecticut. I'm here for your *wife*, who is pregnant with your *child*, my *grandchild*. I'm here to support *her*. I'm not here for *you*."

She says this like I am a steaming pile of poo that she stepped in by mistake, and from the way her eyes regard me, I'm probably not far off-base.

The theater is quiet now, and we're still in a stand-off, my mother's suitcase in her hand, her posture rigid, her face hard. My hands are in the pockets of my jeans and I feel like I'm 10 years old again; like moving, even an inch, would get me a date with my father's belt or a wooden spoon. Faced with her fury, I've instantly regressed, and I can't move.

After an interminable silence, she speaks again, slowly and softly.

"When your father and I got married, I was very young. He was too. We were childhood sweethearts who'd been set up on a date by mutual friends during high school and never moved on or apart from each other after that."

I nod. I know the story.

"It's sweet, isn't it?" she asks.

I nod again.

"But it was *not* always perfect," she says. "There were heartbreaks. There were troubles."

Her eyebrows furrow for a moment, and I wonder briefly about these heartbreaks and troubles, because she and my dad always *seemed* so solid, so perfect.

"Through it all, however, we didn't move on or apart from each other. There were money problems and miscarriages. The deaths of our parents. Three rowdy boys. Sickness. Loss. Fights. Fear. Anger. Times I said, "I hate you," and meant it. Times I said, "I hate you," and didn't." She pauses, then reaches out and places her hand on my forearm, which is crossed over my chest. "We held on no matter what. That's marriage, Joshua."

"I know, Mom," I say, "and I told Courtney that we would talk about everything at—"

"But you're not ready for marriage," she says, speaking over me as though she didn't even hear me. "Not even a little bit. You've cut bait at the first major challenge to come along. You're still a child. A self-centered, egotistical, self-indulgent man-child. And that's a shame because your beautiful, smart wife deserves a man." She cocks her head to the side. "*That's* why I stopped by this theater on my way to Connecticut. Not for *you*, but for *her*. Because I feel very strongly that you should offer your wife a divorce."

I recoil as though slapped, staring at my mother like

she's an alien.

I *know* my parents' stance on divorce. I've known it my whole life. It is the wrongest wrong and evilest evil. It is the breaking of a sacred bond, of a covenant between two people and the God who blessed and ordained their union. There is no place for it in my mother's vernacular, and it's the first time I have ever, in my entire life, heard her advocate for it.

And she is recommending it to me.

"What are you talking about? No one's even mentioned div—"

"Courtney deserves a *man* who can love her and her baby, preferably *before* her baby is born or very close to that time, so that her child will always know the love of a father. A father is crucial to the development of a human being, and Courtney's baby, *my grandbaby*, needs that presence in his or her life."

"Over my dead body."

"In some ways," she says, with tears pooling in her eyes, "it would be better if that were the case. Only because then your absence in your child's life would be explainable, would be understandable, would be forgivable. We could make up stories about how much you loved your wife and how desperately you would have loved your child. Maybe we could even convince ourselves to believe them as time went on."

"I *do* love my—"

"Your wife? No, you don't. And you *certainly* don't deserve her." She blinks her eyes and raises her chin, and she is so unflinching, I am convinced she is made of steel, not bone. "Divorce her, Joshua." With her free hand, she gestures to the theater with a sweeping wave. "*This* is your priority. *This* is what you're married to." Her arm lowers, hanging by her side. "Do the right thing: let Courtney go."

And then, without another word, she turns and walks back up the aisle, through the doors and into the lobby, leaving me alone.

Let Courtney go.

The words reverberate through my head, echoing like they were screamed instead of whispered. Is that what this has come to? Has it escalated *that* quickly? That divorce is now on the table and even being advocated by my own mother?

Let Courtney go. Let Courtney go. Let Courtney go.

I think about her sitting on that barstool so long ago telling me she wants to get married...about holding her in my arms as we danced in the moonlight last spring...about vaulting over a bar and kissing her for the first time on a rainy sidewalk. I think about her face when she saw me waiting at the altar at a little Scottish church...about the way her eyes close when she's on the verge of an orgasm...about the way she laughs, and how she smells like honeysuckle...and the way she says "I love you too."

She is my wife, goddamnit. She is mine and I am hers. Until the end of time. We said the words. We promised.

I promised.

Let Courtney go. Let Courtney go. Let Courtney go.

I set my jaw, which, for the first time in days feels less

like bone and more like steel.

I take a deep breath, letting go of my comforting anger, and allowing my fierce, raging, rabid fear to step forward in all of its shrill and terrifying glory.

Let Courtney go?

The *only* response I have to that profanity, is:

"No."

* * *

On the way home from the theater, I make a detour into Amazon Books, heading to the "Parenting" section. I don't know exactly what I'm looking for. I just hope I recognize it when I see it.

The Expectant Father. No. Too intimidating.

We're Pregnant! God, help me.

Dude, You're Gonna Be a Dad. It's an ugly brownish-purple color in a sea of baby blues and powder pinks. The cover has grayish sperm swimming around and there's mention of a "Freak-out" in the Index. *Yep. This is the one.*

I take it off the shelf and hold it by my side, feeling not unlike my thirteen-year-old self buying a copy of *Playboy* from the local pharmacy. I beeline to the register, pay for it without making eye contact with the clerk because I'm really not ready for the twenty-something female cashier to congratulate me, and get out of here as fast as possible.

My assignment for this weekend? Read this bad boy from cover to cover and then figure out what the fuck comes next.

Do I want a kid?

No. Not really.

Do I want Courtney?

Yes. Absolutely. Positively. No question.

So…do I want a kid?

I guess, because Courtney and the kid are a package deal, *I do.*

I consider taking the bus home, but instead, I decide to walk. It's a long walk and it'll take me over an hour, but I can use that time to think.

I can't lie: seeing my mother has me shook.

It's jolted me out of a crockpot of self-pity and anger, and into a boiling vat of fear.

Until she said the words, I didn't actually think losing Courtney was a possibility…at least not one I'd processed. We've only been apart for a week. She's been in Greenwich, while I've been here. For me, it's been an exercise of feeding my anger and burying my head in the sand about her pregnancy.

But for the first time since our plane trip from hell, I ask myself what this week has been like for her. Rejected by her husband, who hasn't reached out to her once, has she thought of this brief separation as a precursor to divorce? And was my mother acting not just as a conduit to my conscience, but as Courtney's emissary?

Does Courtney want a divorce?

The thought sends a chill down my spine.

It suddenly seems impossible that I didn't consider it.

She is wealthy, beautiful, and has everything going for her. She could easily find someone else to take my place—to love her, care for her, raise my kid, *my child*, with her if I don't, or can't, step up to the plate.

So, the first thing she needs to know is that even though I'm scared shitless of being a dad, and the timing, frankly, isn't great, I'm in. I'm *not* out, as she may believe.

I'm in.

I pull my phone from my back pocket and open a text chat with Courtney.

Hi. How are you feeling? I miss you.

Standing under a streetlight in a light snow, I rub flakes off the screen, my heart lurching when three cycling dots come up. But then it plummets when they disappear without leaving a message for me.

I was shocked on the plane. I said some things I didn't mean. When you're ready, I'd like to talk.

Again, three dots appear, telling me she's reading, but they disappear again without a text back.

I love you, Courtney. Nothing can change that.

I wait and wait, until my screen is wet from all the flakes that have fallen on it. But no dots appear. And no words either.

Fuck.

I've got some work to do.

CHAPTER 10
• CONFLICT RESOLUTION •

"Fight fair. This means giving each other a chance to speak in a way that feels safe for both of you. But more importantly, it means listening with a full and loving heart, free of recriminations and past hurts."

--Dr. Sydney Morningstar

Courtney

My parents mean well.

Their house is comfortable and spacious, their cook makes "healthy mommy" dinners, and I can take a nice walk to and from the beach at any time of the day or night by myself because their neighborhood is so safe.

Joanie, who has been staying with my parents for almost a week now, sits beside my mother in the sun room, commenting on the gorgeous water views, as she knits socks, hats, and blankets for the baby.

In a twist I never saw coming—although perhaps it is due to the fact that all of my mother's hair has fallen out and she refuses to see her high society friends—Miranda Salinger and Joanie Dalton have become best friends. They giggle and chat, sharing a pot of coffee together every morning, and watching "Dr. Phil" every afternoon.

But they also fuss.

Oh my God, do these two fuss over me.

There is a constant stream of advice and questioning—"Put your feet up!", "Are you too close to that screen?", "Did you take your prenatal vitamins?"—that has not only gotten on my nerves, but has shredded them raw.

I'm not carrying the Baby Jesus! I told them yesterday when their well-meaning advice became too much.

Joanie sucked in a sharp breath of shock and my mother told me to watch my mouth. So I took yet another frigid walk out to Greenwich Point, wishing, for the thousandth time, that I was home in New York with my husband rather than here.

After a week of silence, Josh texted me last Friday. Not much. Just a few words about missing me and loving me and wanting to talk. They were sweet words, and I confess I cried tears of relief to know he still loves me, but he didn't mention our baby even once, and I have promised myself that until his language includes both of us, I can't write back to him. Until he is ready to accept and love her, he can't be a part of my life either.

Yes. *Her.*

I'm having a girl.

At my last appointment, Dr. Geiger asked if I wanted to know the sex of my child, and even though tears slid from my eyes, wishing desperately that my husband was standing beside me for such an important moment, I said yes.

When he told me that I was having a girl, I started sobbing, and with no one there to support me, it left the nurse to pat my arm awkwardly until my tears subsided. I have a framed ultrasound picture of my little girl beside my bed, the black and white image so clear, I can see bubbles rising from her tiny mouth. She is alive inside of me, and I love her more than I have ever loved another human being. I rub my stomach as I lie alone in bed and promise her that I will be the best mother I can possibly be.

From the moment the doctor told me her sex, I have been calling her Pippa in my head, which is strange since that's the main character in Josh's play, *Miss Gibbs Will See You Now*, so I've decided to name her Philippa and call her "Pippa." I haven't shared her name with the grandparents yet (*They don't even know she's a she! Shhhh!*) but that's only because I am still hoping that Josh will want to be a part of her life, and these precious details, like her sex and her name, should be shared with him first.

Because I can't stand another moment being fussed over by the "grandmas" I borrow my mother's car on Wednesday afternoon and head into town. There are a few baby boutiques on Greenwich Avenue, and I'm hoping some retail therapy will lift my spirits a little.

An hour later, I'm leaving the third shop, my arms laden with shopping bags, when I run straight into a man entering the shop I'm exiting.

"I'm so sorry!"

"My fault!"

I look up to see Stockard Chase standing before me, a surprised, but growing, smile on his freckled face.

"Courtney Salinger!"

"Stock!"

Two bags slipped from my hands in our collision, but now the rest whoosh to the pavement as Stock pulls me into his arms for a big hug. And it feels so long since I've been held like this, my eyes fill with tears, and I close them, sniffling against his shoulder.

"It's good to see you," he whispers huskily near my ear. "Let me help."

Stock reaches down to collect my various shopping bags, then looks at me with a tender smile. "How about coffee?"

I nod, using my gloves to dab at the corners of my eyes, and giving him a brave smile. "I'd love it."

He ushers me across the street to a little Italian bistro next door to Tiffany's asking the hostess for a table for two, and a moment later, we're sitting by the window, my bags securely by my side and two cappuccinos on the way.

"What are you doing here?" I ask Stock.

"My dad," he says, unwrapping the scarf from around his neck. "He had surgery on his knee this morning up at the hospital."

"Oh, no! I'm sorry. Is everything okay?"

"Of course. They gave him horse tranquilizers for the pain, so he'll be out of it until tomorrow. I thought I'd do a little early Christmas shopping." He grins. "But I think you already bought everything!"

"I got a little carried away," I say. Then, I add impulsively, "I'm expecting."

"Whoa!" His eyes widen, sliding to my belly and back. "That's great, Courts."

I pull off my gloves and lay them on the table. "I'm only seventeen weeks, so I'm not showing yet."

"Dalton must be over the moon, eh?"

I can feel my face fall, and I reach for my napkin, laying it over my lap carefully, fussing with it so I don't have to meet his eyes. I don't know what to say, and I'm so sick and tired of crying.

"Courtney?"

I gulp, looking up at my old friend. "He's...not thrilled."

Stock's eyebrows furrow for a moment, but the waitress returns with our steaming-hot mugs, and we pause in our conversation to thank her.

"Is that why you're here?" asks Stock, blowing on his coffee. "I assumed you were just visiting, but are you two...separated?"

I warm my hands on the glass mug before lifting it to my lips. "Unofficially, I guess. It—it didn't go well when I told him the news. I decided to move home for a while."

"Courts," says Stock, his lips grim, but his eyes warm. "I'm so sorry this has happened."

"Me too," I say softly, taking another sip of the strong, bracing coffee. "Is it really *that* terrifying?"

"Kids?"

"Mmm."

"It'd be easy for me to sit here, as a guy who missed his chance with you, and tell you that your husband's being an asshole," he sighs, giving me a small smile. "But I'd be lying. Kids are terrifying. To most guys. Me included."

"Why?" I ask. "Why do you feel like that?"

"Why does he?"

I shrug, thinking back to our conversations about having children. "He feels like his life will change."

"And it will."

"He doesn't feel ready."

"Sounds about right," says Stock. "Maybe he had a tough childhood?"

I shake my head. "Nope. His parents are awesome. He loves them."

"The truth? It's the ultimate trap," says Stock with a shrug. "A test can prove paternity. You can try to act like it didn't happen, but the courts will still make you pay. You're locked in. For life."

It's the ultimate trap. It's not lost on me that Stock is using the same language Josh used, and in a weird way it makes me feel better that Josh's sentiments probably weren't personal so much as universal.

"But why is that a *bad* thing?" I ask.

"Think about the life of a single guy. Let's say he has a convertible, he screws who he wants, and he spends his money on luxuries like summer shares and trips to Vegas. Suddenly, he's trading in the convertible for a minivan, he's tied to one woman for the rest of his life, and his once-disposable income is no longer his. It's paying for diapers and little sweaters and the wrong kind of toys. It's...change."

I give my friend a look. "Josh didn't have a car, let alone a convertible, he appeared to be perfectly happy screwing only me, and I make most of the money."

"That just makes it worse," he says, a sexy little smile playing on his lips.

"How so?"

"He didn't even have a great car or lots of money. He had you. Now...he doesn't."

"What do you mean? Of course he still has me!"

"No, Courtney. The baby has you. The baby is your priority now."

"But I still love him! I want him to be a part of this with me."

"And he knows that?"

"What do you mean, "he knows that"?"

"When you told him you were pregnant, you told him that you still loved him and still wanted him to screw you?"

"You're being crass."

"I'm being *real*," he insists.

"I saw the way he was with you, both in the Hamptons and at your housewarming, and that guy is crazy about you. Do you understand what he's losing? What this baby is taking away from him? He had this *great* life. A gorgeous wife, who was clearly in love with him. Endless dates. Endless sex. Your eyes lighting up just for him. No responsibilities beyond making you happy. Just settling into an awesome marriage and feeling, every day, like he won the lottery." Stock leans forward, tenting his hands on the table and looking me straight in the eyes. "Do you know how much it must hurt to part with those things?"

"He doesn't have to lose them."

"He already has."

"But it's our child."

"Sure. But you're his wife."

"And I still want to *be* his wife," I cry, exasperated. "I just want to be someone's mother too."

Stock stirs a little sugar into his coffee. "You surprised him, didn't you?"

"What?"

"The baby. It was unplanned?"

I nod. "It was definitely unplanned."

"So he wasn't ready."

"Not at all," I say.

Stock turns his hands so they're palms-up, as if to say, *What did you expect?*

"Are you kidding me?" I demand. "I was surprised too! Our *surprise* was something we could have shared!"

"But—and correct me if I'm wrong, Courts—you wanted it. Either that, or the second you found out you were expecting, you were instantly on board. Which one?"

I take a long sip of coffee. "Both."

"And there it is," says Stock. "You wanted kids. He wasn't ready yet."

"But it doesn't matter," I say. "Pippa's coming. He needs to get on board."

"Pippa?" asks Stock, his smile warm and sweet. "You're having a girl?"

"Oh, shit," I say, shaking my head at the slip. "Josh doesn't even know yet."

"I won't tell him," says Stock, leaning back from me. He tilts his head to the side, regarding me thoughtfully. "You know…"

"What?"

"Nah. Forget it."

"What?" I ask again. "You've sat here for half an hour listening to my problems. Say whatever you want."

"I'm not saying I hope your separation is permanent, Courts, but if it is…" He bites his bottom lip before continuing. "Give me a chance?"

"Stock," I say softly. "I'm not the girl for you."

"You could be."

"I'm not." I shake my head. "Besides, you're terrified of having kids too!"

"True. But I'd try to figure that out. I'd try to accept…Pippa. I'd try to make you happy," he says, straightening up in his seat as he gestures to the waitress for the check. "Offer stands."

We hug outside of the restaurant for a long moment, and Stock kisses me gently on the cheek as a late-afternoon snow begins to fall.

"Thanks for listening," I say. "I owe you one."

He nods. "Take care of yourself, Courtney Salinger."

As I walk back to my mother's car, I think about what Stock said—about how having a baby means losing me… means that I won't want to be his wife, in every sense of the word, anymore. I understand what Stock was saying. I'm not saying I agree with it, because part of me thinks it's ridiculous, but yes, I get it. Josh and I had a great life, and the reality is that we don't know how Pippa is going to change it. Will she make it better? Worse? Complicate it?

Enrich it? All those things at the same time, right? And those things are messy. Life is about to get messy. And I can understand how Josh might not want to jump head-first into a mess. I can—just a little bit—see it from his perspective.

I consider sharing these thoughts to him in a text message, but as I'm placing my bags in the trunk of my mom's car, my phone buzzes. I sit down in the driver's seat, take off my gloves, and open my phone.

It's a text.

From Josh.

Courtney, it's been 11 days since you walked off that plane, which translates to 11 days of hell. I miss you so bad. I think about you all the time. You and the baby. I wonder how you're doing...if you're tired, if you're getting sick...and I'm pissed off at myself for not being there for you.

"Josh," I whisper, my heart swelling at the words, *You and the baby*, because I have needed to see some iteration of them so badly.

Would you be willing to talk to me? Please, baby. I need you.

My fingers fly across the letters.

I'd be willing, I write.

But then my mind slips back to that horrible conversation on the plane when he said so many terrible things. I'm not sure I could handle that again.

Maybe with a marriage counselor? I suggest.

Three dots appear, then disappear. Appear again, then...

Do you feel that's necessary? he asks.

In my mind, I can still hear the words: *All I feel right*

now…is regret. I mewl softly, blinking my eyes like mad. It will take a while for me to get over that pain, to forget how it felt to be so rejected by the man I love more than any other.

Yes, I type. *I think it would be a good idea.*

Just until I am assured that he's not going to hurt me like that again.

Fine, he responds.

I'll text you a date and time, I say.

I stare at the screen, wondering if he'll write again. He does.

I don't have the words to tell you how sorry I am, he says, and now I'm crying, because I needed that apology so badly.

I think of Pippa, of how much she and I need Josh in our lives. I need him to step up now. I need him to prove to me that he's all in, for me, for our baby, for our life together, for our future.

Actions speak louder than words, I type. *Show me.*

***

Josh

I'm late.

I'm fucking late for the most important appointment of my life.

Right now, I am supposed to be sitting next to my wife, meeting with a marriage counselor, at an appointment she booked, that started forty-five minutes ago, and instead, I'm sprinting down the streets of New York like a fucking madman, hoping she's still there when I finally rush through the door an hour late.

Fuck, fuck, fuck, but this is not my fault.

I never take the elevator. Never.

But I had a budget meeting with Simi Frederick and the Emerging Playwrights board at two o'clock on the lower level of the Vivian Beaumont Theater. By three o'clock I was getting itchy. Even though Courtney had thoughtfully chosen a marriage counselor only ten minutes from the theater, the appointment was booked for three-thirty and I wanted to be there a little early, just to prove to her how important this is to me. At three-ten, I told the board I needed to leave, and they were gracious about my exit, praising my progress on the play and sharing their high hopes for a great show.

I walked out of the meeting room, and there it was: the fucking elevator. Waiting for me. Promising a swift ride to the main floor.

I pressed the button, the door opened, I stepped inside.

And then?

Nothing.

No sounds. No movements. Nothing.

I pressed every button. I pulled the CALL/HELP button repeatedly.

Finally, a fuzzy voice came on over the intercom saying that the mechanics were jammed, but they were sending someone with a crowbar to open the doors for me.

Ten minutes passed. Twenty. Thirty. By three forty-five, I was picturing Courtney looking at her clock, texting me, even calling me, but I was stuck in a metal box on the lower level of a concrete building. Nothing was getting through.

Fuck, fuck, fuck, I screamed. Pulling the CALL/HELP button again, I demanded that the operator get me the fuck out of there. He shared that the technician was on his way and asked for my patience.

So there I was.

Sitting on the floor of an elevator.

And I could see my whole life—everything that mattered most to me—slipping away.

Since last Friday, I have read *Dude, You're Gonna Be A Dad* three times, cover-to-cover, and I feel like I am ready to make a fresh start with my wife. I am ready to support Courtney through the next twenty-four weeks of her pregnancy with ice cream and pickles, foot rubs, and ultrasound appointments. I am ready—or at least ready to *try*—to embrace the concept of fatherhood in a real and personal way.

Since I allowed my fears to take center stage, and with the help of my new book, I've come to a few conclusions:

1. Yes. My life, as I know it, is about to change.

2. No. That change doesn't have to be terrible.

3. It's up to me if I show up or don't.

Regardless of how I felt on the plane two weeks ago, Courtney didn't "trap" me into anything. We got pregnant by mistake, but that's our reality. And I have a choice: I can walk or I can stay. And faced with the prospect of losing my wife and child? It's a no brainer for me, just like it was when I raced off to Scotland to marry Courtney: that woman and that baby are mine. They're *my* people, *my* family, and I'll be damned if I let them go because I'm afraid to be a dad. I'll just have to learn *how* to be a dad, and trust that Courtney will be there for me all along the way.

Finally, the guy with the crowbar got there and wedged the doors open. I crawled through a two-foot opening, raced up the stairs, and now, here I am, running like the devil's on my heels, across West 65th and up Central Park West to 74th Street. Huffing and puffing, I turn left, looking for number 10 and flinging open the double glass doors of an office building. A doorman rises from his seat at a desk, surprised by my sudden and flustered appearance.

"Sir? Can I—"

"Dr. Scott! Where is—"

"Second floor. Third door on the right."

I eye the elevator, then turn back to the doorman. "Do you have stairs?"

I take them two at a time, bursting onto the second floor and running down the hall. It was after four when I left Lincoln Center. It's got to be close to four-thirty by now. I find the marriage counselor's door, but it's locked, and I bang on the door loudly, yelling, "Dr. Scott? Are you there?"

It's quiet for a moment, and I lean against the wall beside the door, clenching my teeth together as my chest rises and falls from my desperate run.

I've missed her and he's gone home for the day.

Fuck.

Pulling my phone from my back pocket, I see that Courtney tried to call me three times and left several texts. I'm sure she thought I'd decided not to come, that I'd decided to turn my back on my wife and child, and regret rises up in me, so strong, so bitter, that I can barely stand it. I shove off from the wall, heading for the stairs, trying to think how I can possibly make amends for this massive fuck-up, when the door opens.

"Mr. Dalton, by any chance?"

I turn around, stepping back to the office as my vision blurs from tears. "That's me."

"You're late," he says. "Is everything alright?"

"I got stuck," I say, running my hands through my hair. "An elevator—it broke down, and I—I waited for a crowbar, but I was late. I ran here. I'm sorry. She's gone. I know she's gone, but—"

"She's still here," he says, opening the door a little wider to reveal Courtney—my Courtney, standing behind him.

And this is the real miracle of my wife.

She steps around the doctor and runs—races—into my arms. And I have never been so grateful, not in my entire life, for the gift of second chances. She is crying. And I am crying. And we are holding on to each other so tightly it should hurt, but it doesn't. It feels miraculous. It feels like God is embracing us while we embrace each other. And in that moment, I pledge to do everything I can to make this woman happy, to keep our child safe, to make sure that my family is always this whole.

I lean away, reaching for her face and cupping her cheeks in my hands.

"I love you," I say. "I didn't mean any of it. I was just

scared."

"I surprised you," she answers. "I should have figured out a better way to tell you."

"I read a parenting book. I read it three times. I can do this, Court. I promise. I can be a father. I'm going to try my best, baby. I promise."

"That's all I can ask for," she says, leaning up on tiptoes to press her lips to mine. "I missed you so much, Josh. I love you too."

"How are you?" I ask, ignoring the tears that snake down my cheeks. "How are you feeling?"

"Good." She sobs softly. "It's…it's a girl, Josh."

I flashback to the dream I had the night we made this child—the image of a little blonde girl with blue eyes, just like Courtney's—and I know that dream was no fluke, no figment of my imagination. It was my daughter's soul telling mine that she was coming, that she would be here soon.

"I can't wait to meet her," I say.

"I've been calling her Pippa," says Courtney, half crying and half laughing. "Like the character in *Miss*—"

"*Gibbs Will See You Now*," we finish together.

We have both forgotten that Dr. Scott is standing in the doorway beside us until he clears his throat. "You two don't need therapy."

"We don't?" asks Courtney.

He shakes his head. "Nope. You're going to be just fine."

Courtney reaches out her hand, placing it on his arm. "Thank you, Dr. Scott."

"Be well, Mrs. Dalton," he answers, handing her a coat and purse, and closing his office door with a soft click.

"Mrs. Dalton," I say, pulling my wife back into my arms. "That's music to my ears."

"Mine too," she says, grinning up at me. "I missed you so much."

"You too, baby," I say, leaning down to kiss her sweet lips again. "When did you find out? About...Pippa?"

"Just this week," she says. She bites her lower lip and her smile fades a touch. "Are you sure, Josh? Are you sure you want this?"

"I want *you*," I say. "I want *Pippa*." I take her hand and lead her toward the elevator, because, frankly, I don't care if we get trapped in one together. "I don't know what kind of dad I'll be, but you're...you're my girls. I want you home with me."

She looks away from me for a second, and it's just enough to make me worry.

"Hey," I say, running my knuckles over her cheek, "will you come home tonight?"

I can see that she's hesitant. And I understand. When I think back to the things I said to her on the plane, it makes me hate myself. Undoubtedly, she needs time to heal from that hurt, and though I want her by my side, I can give her that time and space if she needs it.

"Listen," I say, trying a different angle, "come home for a little bit. For a few hours. I'll make mint tea and we can talk. And you can call a car service to take you back to Greenwich later if you feel like it. Okay?"

She gives me a small smile, and it hurts a little, but at least she says, "Okay."

***

The last message Courtney sent to me, aside from the date, time, and location of the counseling session, told me that actions speak louder than words and to "show" her that I was sorry for what I said to her.

In an effort to show her that I took her advice seriously, I have worked on a little project after rehearsal over the last three nights. It's been backbreaking and exhausting, but I'm hoping that it proves to her that I am serious about both my apology, and my intentions to be a good husband and father.

When we get to our apartment, I kiss her hand before letting it go.

"Wait here for a second?"

"In the hallway?"

I nod, holding up a finger. "Just one second. I promise!"

I slip into the apartment and light the candles I've left on the foyer table, on the bar in the kitchen, on the coffee table and bookcases in the living room, and finally, the little votives on the floor, lining the back hallway.

When I go back to the front door and open it, her eyes are wide, but at least she's grinning. "What are you up to in there? Throwing your dirty clothes into the laundry?"

"Something else. Come on."

I pull her into the apartment.

"It's so pretty in here! Candles everywhere!" she

whispers, holding my hand as I tug her into the living room. On the coffee table is my new book, and she glances at it. "Is that the one you read?"

I nod. "It was exactly what I needed."

"I'm so proud of you," she says. "I know you didn't want this. I know this has been hard for you. It means so much to me that you're trying, Josh."

"Come on," I say. "There's more."

"Candles in the bedroom?" she asks, her voice lowering a little, like it does when she's turned on.

"Mm-hm," I say, "and somewhere else too."

I stop in the hallway and look down at her beautiful face, lit softly by candlelight.

"I have no idea what kind of dad I'll be, Court," I tell her, reaching to place one palm on her sweater, over her slightly-swollen stomach. When she covers it with hers, my heart flip-flops in the best, most amazing way. "But I promise you—*I promise you*—that I don't now, and never will, regret a single moment I have spent with you. I love you." I press my hand against her lightly. "I promise to love her too."

Her eyes glisten in the candlelight as she sniffles softly, putting her arms around my neck and kissing me. Her satiny tongue slides against mine, and I find myself hardening against her, wanting her so much after the torture of two weeks spent apart.

"I've missed this so much," she sighs, arching against me, cradling my hardness with her softness. "I want you."

"Stay here tonight?" I ask.

She nods. "Yes. I'm staying forever."

My body is on fire for her and I can't wait to get her into our bed, but I have one last thing to share with her first. Drawing away from her, I turn the knob on the guest room door and push it open.

"Take a look."

She tilts her head to the side, looking at me curiously before stepping through the doorway. The walls are freshly-painted a soft yellow, and I've had plush, cream-colored, wall-to-wall carpet installed. A white crib has been assembled on one side of the room, and a pale-yellow gliding rocker with matching ottoman wait at the ready nearby. A changing table with a butter-colored terrycloth cover sits across the room from the crib, and a matching white dresser is ready to be filled with baby clothes.

I used our money—our little nest egg—to furnish this room, and I hope my wife loves it as much as I do.

"I put the old furniture in basement storage," I say. When she doesn't speak, I feel a little nervous and ramble on. "You told me to show you…and so I—I—"

When she turns around, her cheeks are wet. "You did all of this?"

"Yeah." My eyes are tearing up too. "You can change anything you want to…I didn't know if we were having a boy or a girl, but I wanted—"

"I love it. I love everything. I love you!"

She steps forward, pressing her body against mine, twining her arms around my neck and kissing me like the world is ending. Or beginning, maybe. Yeah. Maybe this is day one of a whole new world, I think, pulling my wife into my arms and kissing her back with everything I am, with everything I have, with everything I ever hope to be.

I hold on.

She holds on.

We hold on.

EPILOGUE
The following summer

• FOREVER •

"There is no one tried-and-true recipe for forever. Every couple must make their own mistakes and share their own triumphs. But if I were to give one piece of advice, it would be this: stay together. The grass is most likely not greener elsewhere, and if you and your spouse have once shared love, you should always be able to figure out how to love again. Besides, you can't have a happily-ever-after unless you are still together at THE END."

--Dr. Sydney Morningstar

<u>Josh</u>

"It doesn't matter if you win or lose," says Courtney, reaching for my hand and gripping it tightly during the five-minute intermission. "You were nominated. A first-run play. By a brand-new playwright. In the first-year of production."

I lean to the left and press my lips to hers quickly. "And it's not a musical."

"And it's not a musical!" she exclaims. "A play. Selling out every night. That's...that's..."

I kiss her again. "Amazing."

"Amazing," she agrees. "Do you know the stats on that?"

"Nope. But I feel sure you're about to share them."

"An original play. Written by an unknown playwright. *Not* a revival. With no Hollywood talent…"

I wait because when Courtney's nerves take over and she starts quoting statistics to me, the payoff is always pretty sweet.

"I have no stats," she says.

"What? Impossible."

"Possible," she insists. "There's no collected data for a situation like this, Josh. You're a unicorn."

"I am?"

"You are." She nods earnestly, scanning my eyes. "*My* unicorn."

My phone buzzes, and I drop my wife's hand to answer it. "Hello?"

"Hi, there. Is it intermission?"

"Yeah. How's everything going?" My mom and Miranda Salinger are watching the Drama Desk Awards from Courtney's and my apartment, where they're babysitting Pippa tonight.

"Is that your mom?" whispers Courtney, pulling the phone from my hand. "Joanie? How's she doing? … She took the bottle? … Oh, good. … Uh-huh. … The rocker's probably best. In the nursery. … My mom knows where I keep them. … Thank you for everything. …Here he is."

While my wife talks to my mother about our daughter, I can picture everything that's happening at home: the warm, sweet smell of our daughter's nursery, the way Pippa gurgles before belching, the light weight of my daughter's precious body in my arms as she falls asleep after eating.

I didn't know.

That's what I would tell anyone who asked why I was so scared, why I was so against kids, why I gave my beloved, rockstar wife such a hard time when she told me she was pregnant.

I didn't know.

I didn't know that when I looked into Pippa's eyes for the first time, that I would fall in love for the second time in my life.

I didn't know that when I fell asleep beside my wife, with our sleeping daughter between us, that I would feel a wholeness, a completeness, that I had never known before.

I didn't know that being a father would come so easily, so naturally, and that it would become my new favorite job.

I didn't know that my wife's body, which carried our child, would curve and swell in the most awe-inspiring ways.

I didn't know how much a human heart could expand.

I didn't know how messy and full and beautiful life could be until that day. I didn't know how much I was missing until I had it all.

And now that I do, all I can say is "Thank you."

To God.

To the universe.

To grace.

To fate.

To Courtney, who – once upon a time – sat down on a barstool, ordered a gimlet, and told me she wanted to get married.

"Josh," she whispers, nudging me with my phone as the orchestra plays a few bars of back-to-the-show music.

"Mom," I say. "Kiss Pips. Love you three. Gotta go."

"Good luck, son!" she says. "We're watching! We're rootin' for ya!"

I hang up and pocket my phone, taking Courtney's hand and pulling it onto my knee as the lights dim. *Calm down, Josh. Calm down. You're not going to win.*

"You might," whispers Courtney, close to my ear.

"Might?"

"Win."

"It's an honor just to be nominated," I tell her, staring at the stage as Michael Urie approaches the microphone.

"This year, the nominees for Drama Desk Best Newcomer includes two actors, an actress, a lighting designer, and a director. And the nominees are: Jack Capp, King Lear, *King Lear.*" Urie pauses for applause before continuing. "Henry Edwards, David, *Goliath's Side.*" More applause. "Sara Conwys, Elizabeth Bennet, *Austen's Pride.*" A few whoops from the balcony for Shelby. "Audie Matte, Lighting Design, *Tequila Mockingbird.*" A brief clap for a less popular category, and finally… "And, Josh Dalton, Director, *Miss Gibbs Will See You Now.*" The applause is generous as Courtney's fingers grip mine so tightly, I'm fairly certain she's cutting off the blood supply. "And the Drama Desk award for Best Newcomer goes to… Josh Dalton, Director, *Miss Gibbs Will See You Now!*"

The theater erupts into applause as Courtney gasps beside me, turning to face me with a huge smile and tears running down her cheeks.

"It's you!" she says. "You did it!"

Cupping her face, I kiss her quickly before standing up and making my way down the long aisle to the stage.

My God. My God. *Miss Gibbs*...won.

As I walk up the five stairs, I realize I'm shaking, and worried I'll drop the heavy glass trophy, I set it down on the podium as Michael Urie hugs me, clapping me on the back and telling me he wants a role in my next show.

Finally, it's just me at the podium, with bright lights in my face. So bright, I can barely make out my wife's face in the back of the theater. But I shield my eyes and squint, and there she is: my wife, my love, my Courtney, blinking back tears with her hands clasped under her chin.

"Th-thank you, Michael," I say, clearing my throat before continuing. "Thank you to the New York critics, to Drama Desk, and to the Emerging Playwrights Competition. Thank you to Simi Frederick, to Lincoln Center, and to my production team." I am on autopilot now, thanking the actors who've brought my characters to life and the vast crew that have been with me since opening night at Lincoln Center. But as my lips form words and my voice speaks them, I'm staring at Courtney, who is my everything, without whom I would be half the man I am today.

"During the production of *Miss Gibbs Will See You Now*, at Lincoln Center, my wife, Courtney, was pregnant with our first child. I actually missed the opening night of *Miss Gibbs* on Broadway because Courtney went into labor. Our Pippa, who is two months old today, was born during the curtain call." There's a light smattering of laughter in the audience. "Best curtain call I ever missed." I imagine my mother, mother-in-law, and daughter at home, cuddled on the couch together, watching me as I accept this award. "We've had an unconventional love story, my wife and me. Maybe someday I'll write about it." My eyes are full of tears now, as I acknowledge the bounty of my life, the goodness of it and the best thing about it is sitting in Row R, smiling at me with all the love in her heart. And me? I can't, for the life of me, look away. I never want to. When I look up, for the rest of my life, the first thing I want to see…is her.

"Never stop looking at the person you love," I say, my voice choking just a touch on the word love.

"Believe in happy endings. I do."

I grin at my wife, at the woman who has given me everything, and through the glare of light, her eyes steadfastly hold mine.

"And never, ever stop holding on," I say, holding up my trophy as I finish my speech, ready to return to my seat beside the love of my life.

"As a wise woman once said, "You can't have a happily-ever-after unless you're still together at

THE END."

ALSO AVAILABLE
from Katy Regnery

a modern fairytale
(A collection)

The Vixen and the Vet
Never Let You Go
Ginger's Heart
Dark Sexy Knight
Don't Speak
Shear Heaven
Fragments of Ash
At First Sight (coming 2019)
Swan Song (coming 2019)

THE BLUEBERRY LANE SERIES

THE ENGLISH BROTHERS
(Blueberry Lane Books #1–7)

Breaking Up with Barrett
Falling for Fitz
Anyone but Alex
Seduced by Stratton
Wild about Weston
Kiss Me Kate
Marrying Mr. English

THE WINSLOW BROTHERS
(Blueberry Lane Books #8–11)

Bidding on Brooks
Proposing to Preston
Crazy about Cameron
Campaigning for Christopher

THE ROUSSEAUS
(Blueberry Lane Books #12–14)

Jonquils for Jax
Marry Me Mad
J.C. and the Bijoux Jolis

THE STORY SISTERS
(Blueberry Lane Books #15–17)

The Bohemian and the Businessman
The Director and Don Juan
Countdown to Midnight

<u>THE SUMMERHAVEN SERIES</u>

Fighting Irish
Smiling Irish
Loving Irish
Catching Irish

THE ARRANGED DUO

Arrange Me
Arrange Us

STAND-ALONE BOOKS:

After We Break
(a stand-alone second-chance romance)

Frosted
(a stand-alone romance novella for mature readers)

Unloved, a love story
(a stand-alone suspenseful romance)

Under the paranormal pen name
K. P. Kelley

It's You, Book 1
It's You, Book 2

Under the YA pen name
Callie Henry

A Date for Hannah

ABOUT THE AUTHOR

 *New York Times* and *USA Today* bestselling author **Katy Regnery** started her writing career by enrolling in a short story class in January 2012. One year later, she signed her first contract, and Katy's first novel was published in September 2013.

Over forty books and three RITA® nominations later, Katy claims authorship of the multititled Blueberry Lane series. the A Modern Fairytale collection, the Summerhaven series, the Arranged duo, and several other standalone romances, including the critically-acclaimed contemporary romance, *Unloved, a love story.*

Katy's books are available in English, French, German, Italian, Polish, Portuguese, and Turkish.

COMING IN 2019:

At First Sight (inspired by "Aladdin")
Swan Song (inspired by "The Ugly Duckling)

www.ingramcontent.com/pod-product-compliance
Lightning Source LLC
Chambersburg PA
CBHW061132200626
46817CB00016B/1157